Mostly Ghostly

Little Camp of Horrors

4

Experience all the chills of the Mostly Ghostly series!

R.L. STINE

DELACORTE PRESS
A PARACHUTE PRESS BOOK

Published by
Delacorte Press
an imprint of
Random House Children's Books
a division of Random House, Inc.
New York

Visit us on the Web! www.randomhouse.com/kids
Educators and librarians, for a variety of teaching tools, visit us at
www.randomhouse.com/teachers

Library of Congress Cataloging-in-Publication Data is available
upon request.

ISBN: 0-385-74666-0 (trade)
0-385-90916-0 (lib. bdg.)

Printed in the United States of America

January 2005

10 9 8 7 6 5 4 3 2 1

BVG

i

Dear Mom and Dad,

Camp is awesome. Today I won an archery tournament. And I swam from one side of the lake to the other. I'm learning the butterfly stroke, and I'm getting good at diving off the pier.

The older campers are waterskiing, and I can't wait to take lessons.

The guys in my cabin are awesome.

We do some pretty crazy things, like hide in the woods and stay out all night. But our counselor is really cool about it. He thinks we're cool too.

I've made a lot of new friends. And we're all going to e-mail each other and stay in touch after camp is over.

The food is great, especially on barbecue night. Would you believe I ate _six_ hot dogs last night? I guess I worked up a good appetite going on that six-mile hike.

That's about it for now. The guys are calling me to a big tetherball battle.

Please send candy bars. We really need
them. And please send me a little money,
too, so I can buy stuff at the
canteen.

I miss you. Bye for now,

Max

Nice letter home from camp, right?

Well, if you think it's for real, you're majorly crazy. It's a joke. *No way* would yours truly, Max Doyle, write a letter like that.

For one thing, I *hate* summer camp. Why go a hundred miles away? You can get mosquito bites in your own backyard! Being outside all day could give you sunburn or sun poisoning or sunstroke— or something even worse.

For another thing, my parents sent me to Camp Snake Lake. One of the scariest places on earth. A pit of horrors—no kidding. I mean, what does the name tell you? Camp Snake Lake. Does that sound like Camp Smiley Face?

My other problem is that I'm haunted.

I'm haunted by Nicky and Tara Roland, two

ghosts who used to live in my house. I'm the only one who can see and hear them. They're all alone, and they need me to help find their parents.

It's all their fault that I had to go to Camp Snake Lake.

I would have stayed home all summer. I never would have gone away—if it wasn't for them.

I never would have faced the horde of evil ghosts, those ugly, terrifying ghosts. I never would have taken the plunge—into Snake Lake.

And three guesses why they call it that?

Well, believe me, I never wrote any sweet letters home from camp. I didn't have time.

The only letters I wrote were "S.O.S." *Help!!!*

2

IT ALL STARTED IN JULY. My brother Colin was in his room, packing his trunk for camp. He's a big shot junior counselor at Camp Snake Lake.

He loves it there.

What does Colin love about summer camp? Well, he enjoys dunking kids' heads underwater. And scaring the little campers with ghost stories. Tossing kids out of canoes and telling them there's a man-eating crocodile in the water. Hiding dead beetles in the potato salad. Fun things like that.

Colin is big and blond, good-looking and athletic, smart and popular.

In other words, he's a total jerk.

At least, that's my opinion.

I'm not like my older brother. I told my parents I wouldn't go to camp. I said I wanted to stay home, hang out with my friend Aaron, and have fun on my own.

I wanted to practice my magic act. I have a whole bunch of new tricks I want to learn. And I've gotten into word games in a major way.

I do all the puzzle books with word searches and anagrams. Do you know what an anagram is? It's when you take a word or a name and switch all the letters around to make new words.

For example, do you know an anagram for my name—Max E. Doyle?

It's YODEL EXAM.

And do you know an anagram for *Bob*?

It's BOB. Ha ha!

Aaron and I are also building our own Web site. We don't know what it's about yet. But we know it's going to be totally cool.

So there's plenty to do around home. That's what I told my parents. Mom said I need more fresh air. She said I need to build my body by playing sports.

Dad called me a spineless wimp. He's big as a truck and tough, and he always talks like that. I'm used to it. He thinks he can encourage me by calling me a lot of names.

I told him that an anagram for *spineless* is SLIPS SEEN. He just stared at me like I was crazy.

So now they were in Colin's room helping him pack. And I was in my room down the hall, practicing some card tricks. And a voice behind me said, "Hey, Max. What's up?"

Startled, I dropped the deck of cards all over

the floor. I turned and saw Nicky and Tara standing behind me.

They're both tall and thin and have dark hair and gray-green eyes. Nicky is my age—eleven. He wore a black T-shirt and shorts. Tara is nine. She wore a blue sleeveless top over faded low-rise jeans. Red plastic earrings dangled from her ears.

"Why did you sneak up on me like that?" I demanded.

"We're ghosts," Tara said. "We can't help it."

"Can we search one more time?" Nicky asked, peeking under my bed.

"What for?" I said. "We've been searching for months. We've torn this room upside down. The pendant isn't here."

Tara sighed. "We can't give up, Max. We have to keep looking everywhere. If Mom and Dad are inside that pendant . . ." Her voice broke.

Nicky dropped to his stomach and crawled under the bed. "I don't see it," he said.

"Nicky, we've searched every dust ball," I said.

"Maybe there are some new dust balls we haven't searched," Nicky replied.

Tara opened my closet door and began tossing all the junk out of my closet. "That pendant is close by," she said. "I just have a feeling."

I'd better explain.

When my family moved into this house, it was

empty. On the floor in my bedroom, Mom found a silver, bullet-shaped pendant. She put it on a chain and told me to wear it around my neck for good luck.

A few months ago, the ghosts and I learned that the pendant is actually a life pod. Ghosts can live inside it. Nicky and Tara believe their mom and dad are trapped inside the pendant I wear. And maybe we could let them out.

There's only one little problem. I'm not wearing the pendant. It's lost. It's been lost for months.

Where did it go? I don't have a clue.

But of course Nicky and Tara are desperate to find it. They need to find their parents. You see, they don't know what happened to all of them. When they turned up at my house last October, Nicky and Tara couldn't remember how they became mostly ghostly.

I feel so bad for them. One minute they were normal kids. The next minute they were ghosts. No place to live. No parents.

And to make matters worse, an evil ghost showed up. A terrifying ghost named Phears. He wanted to capture Nicky and Tara—and their parents. He still does.

I know Phears is out there somewhere. We have to find Nicky and Tara's parents before he does. And that's why we keep searching for the life pod.

We've torn apart every room in the house—even Colin's room when he was away at a track meet.

No luck.

I think it's lost for good. But they won't give up.

"Help me, Max," Nicky called. We tilted back my couch and looked underneath it. I saw two dimes and a quarter under there, but no pendant.

Tara had finished searching the closet. Now she moved to my bed. "Maybe it's caught between the mattress and the headboard," she said.

She grabbed the pillows and started to heave them off the bed.

"Max!" I heard Mom cry. She stepped into the doorway just as Tara tossed the pillows.

Mom saw my pillows appear to fly into the air by themselves.

"Max!" she cried, pressing her hands to her face. "What is going on?"

3

I HAD TO THINK FAST. "Uh . . . I'm practicing for a pillow fight with Colin," I said.

"But those pillows—they were flying by *themselves*!" Mom cried.

"Of course," I said. "They're *feather* pillows."

I know. It didn't make any sense. But Mom didn't want to talk about pillows.

She stepped over the clutter on the floor. "Max, please change your mind," she said. "Go to summer camp with Colin. He's leaving in a few minutes with the other junior counselors. Let me pack you up."

"No way," I said, crossing my arms over my chest. "I told you. I'm allergic to trees. I can't help it. Even if I see a tree in a movie, I break out in spots."

"That can't be true," Colin said, bursting into my room. "Because you were *born* in a tree!"

Dad came in right behind him. He laughed at Colin's stupid joke.

"At least I was born, not dredged from a swamp," I said to Colin.

No one laughed at that.

No one ever laughs at my jokes.

Mom brushed a hand through my hair. "You don't have to go with Colin. You can take the bus tomorrow with the regular campers."

"Forget it," I muttered. "I can't go to camp. Fresh air makes me cough."

Dad shook his head and scowled at me. "How do you plan to spend your summer, Max? Doing stupid card tricks in your bedroom?"

I picked up a deck of cards from my bed table. "Here. Pick a card, any card."

Colin grabbed a puzzle magazine and flipped through it. "Check this out. *One Hundred and One Anagrams*. And he's worked them all."

He pinched my cheek really hard. "Like to waste time, Maxie?"

I grabbed the magazine out of his hand. "Know what an anagram of *Colin* is?" I asked. "It's *stupid*."

"Please don't fight," Mom said. She said that at least a hundred times a day. Mom is tiny like a little bird, with a quiet little voice, and she doesn't like yelling.

Dad took the deck of cards from me. "You have to get over your fears, Max," he said. "Summer camp will help you."

"I'm not afraid," I replied. "I just don't want to go!"

"Colin will be there to protect you," Mom said.

"Yeah, you got that right." Colin grinned at me. "Know what I'll protect you from? I'll protect you from gut punches. Like this!"

He punched me so hard in the stomach, I thought his hand went out my back! I doubled over, holding my aching gut, groaning like a dying seal.

Mom hurried over to me. "Colin, why did you do that to Maxie?" she asked.

Colin grinned again. "For fun?"

"Unnnnk unnnk," I moaned.

Colin turned to Dad. "I know why Max won't come to my camp. He's afraid he might have to swim in Snake Lake. I told him how it's filled with deadly poisonous snakes."

"That would toughen him up," Dad said.

"No one has ever come out of Snake Lake alive," Colin said, lowering his voice and trying to sound scary.

I shuddered. I guess he *did* sound scary.

"And get this," Colin said to Dad. "When I told Max the story of the Headless Camper, he almost wet his pants."

Dad and Colin both hee-hawed.

"You're a liar!" I cried.

"Stop scaring Maxie with those awful camp stories," Mom scolded.

"It doesn't matter," I said. "I'm not going. No way."

We heard a horn honk out on the street.

"The bus!" Colin cried. "It's here!"

Dad and I grabbed Colin's bags. Then we all hurried downstairs to load him onto the bus. I suddenly felt very happy. A whole summer without Colin! Now, *that's* a vacation!

The bus driver came out to help with the bags. Inside the small yellow school bus, three or four other guys about Colin's age stared out at us. The bus said CAMP NAKE AKE on the side. Someone had pulled off some of the letters.

Mom hugged Colin. Dad hugged him too. Then he and Dad touched knuckles.

Colin started to climb onto the bus. Halfway up the steps, he turned to me. He pulled something out from under his Camp Snake Lake T-shirt.

It glittered in the sunlight.

The pendant!

Colin was wearing the pendant!

"Hey, Max—check out my new good-luck pendant!" he called, a big grin on his face.

"But that's *mine*!" I shouted.

"I'm tossing it to the snakes in Snake Lake! See ya!"

He disappeared into the bus, and it roared away.

4

A FEW MINUTES LATER, I sat on the edge of my bed, feeling glum. Nicky and Tara and I spent *months* searching for that pendant. And stupid Colin had it the whole time.

How could I tell my two ghost friends the bad news?

The house was silent. Mom and Dad had gone to a movie. I think they were seeing *Scream and Die 3*.

They both love totally violent movies with fighting and killing, and people thrown through plate glass windows, and guys screaming and dying hideous deaths every minute. Mom likes them even more than Dad. Go figure.

Well, I felt pretty violent myself. I wanted to *strangle* my brother.

But Colin was gone. Gone for eight long weeks. And we *had* to get that pendant.

"Nicky? Tara? Where are you?" I called, glancing around my room.

No answer.

14

They had disappeared when Mom burst into my room.

"Hey, guys? Are you here? I need to tell you something."

No reply.

I climbed to my feet and started to pace back and forth. I had to calm down and stop feeling so angry. But how?

I called Aaron's house. His mother answered and said Aaron wasn't allowed to come to the phone. He was grounded because he'd played a joke on his little sister.

Aaron had told his sister he had barfed in her bed. It was only potato salad. But when she saw the yellow pile on her blanket, she freaked and puked all over the floor.

"Aaron can come to the phone in about a month," his mom said.

I clicked off the phone and started pacing again. Then I picked up the deck of cards and shuffled it for a while. I practiced shuffling up and shuffling down. The trick is to keep the same five cards on top no matter how many times you shuffle the deck.

I'm getting pretty good at it. But shuffling cards didn't take my mind off Colin and the pendant.

"Nicky? Tara?" I called. "Where *are* you?"

The doorbell rang.

I jumped. I could hear my dog, Buster—our

huge furry wolfhound—barking his head off in the garage. Doorbells drive him crazy. I don't have a clue why.

The front door was open. I saw a man and a woman through the screen door. I blinked. Why did they look familiar?

The man was tall and thin and had wavy brown hair, thinning in front. He had serious brown eyes and a nice smile. He wore a white polo shirt over baggy khakis.

The woman had lighter hair, cut short and straight. Her eyes were blue. They kept darting from side to side. She didn't smile. Instead, she was chewing the pink lipstick off her lips.

She wore a pale pink top over a flowered skirt with lots of pleats.

The man stared at me through the screen door. "I'm sorry to bother you," he said. "We're the Rolands. We used to live in your house. And we're searching for our two kids, Nicky and Tara."

5

"HUH?"

I could feel my eyes popping out of my head. My knees buckled, and I staggered back against the wall.

"You—you—" I struggled to form words.

Nicky and Tara's parents! They were here! They weren't trapped inside the pendant after all.

Of course I recognized them. I had stared at Nicky and Tara's framed snapshot of their parents a hundred times.

And now they stared tensely through the screen door at me. Mrs. Roland held tightly to her husband's arm.

"They're here," I finally managed to say. "Nicky and Tara. I mean, I *know* them. I mean, they're here!"

I could barely hear my voice over the pounding of my heart. I felt so happy and excited, I wanted to *scream*.

"Oh, thank goodness!" Mrs. Roland cried. Tears rolled down her pink cheeks. She gripped Mr. Roland's arm harder, squeezing it tightly.

They both let out long sighs.

"C-come in," I stammered. I pushed open the screen door so they could step inside.

They glanced around. "Everything is so . . . different," Mrs. Roland said. Her voice trembled. "So many memories."

They walked into the living room, holding on to each other. "Yes, it's all so different," Mr. Roland agreed, shaking his head.

"I'll try to find Nicky and Tara," I said. "They won't believe you're finally here."

"It's taken us so long," Mrs. Roland said. She turned her head. I guess she didn't want me to see her cry.

"They've been searching for you this whole time," I told the Rolands. "I . . . I helped too. But . . ."

"Are they here? Where are they?" Mr. Roland asked.

"Upstairs, I think," I said. "Please . . . sit down."

My legs were shaky as I pulled myself up to my room. "Nicky? Tara? You've *got* to appear!" I screamed. "Where are you? *Please*—where are you?"

I felt a whoosh of cold air—and Nicky and Tara popped up in front of me.

"Max? What's wrong?" Tara asked.

"Nothing is wrong!" I cried happily. "They're here. Your parents! They're downstairs!" I was jumping up and down with excitement.

Nicky and Tara flickered in and out of view. Their faces filled with shock, then joy. I could see that their excitement was making them appear, bright and solid, and then fade and disappear like fireflies at night.

Finally, Tara grabbed my arm. "You're not joking? Mom and Dad—they're really downstairs?"

I nodded.

Crying out happily, they both ran from my bedroom. I followed them down the stairs.

By the time I reached the bottom, they were hugging their parents. Everyone was crying. Everyone was talking at the same time.

All four of them had their arms wrapped around each other in a massive tight hug. They moved around and around in a circle, holding each other.

I felt my cheeks. Wet. I was crying too.

Well, how could I help it? I mean, Nicky and Tara hadn't seen their parents in so long.

And now here they were. They just walked up to the front door, and here they were.

Finally, the hug broke. All four of them took a step back, breathing hard. They wiped tears from their cheeks. They were laughing and crying at the same time.

His arms around Nicky and Tara, Mr. Roland smiled at me. "Thank you for being their friend," he said.

Then Tara turned to her mom and dad. "I have a million questions," she said. And she began to ask them. "What happened to us? Why are we ghosts? Did someone kill us? Where have you been all this time?"

6

MRS. ROLAND LAUGHED. "Tara, not so fast. Not so fast!"

"We'll answer all your questions," Mr. Roland said. "It's a long story. But don't worry. We'll explain everything." He stuck out his hand. "But quick—give us the pendant."

"We really have to hurry," their mom said, glancing at the front door. She turned back to them. "Which one of you is wearing it?"

"Max was wearing it the whole time," Nicky said.

Both parents moved quickly across the room to me. "Could we have it back, Max?" Mr. Roland asked. "It's the master life pod. We need it to capture any other ghosts who might come after us."

Mrs. Roland sighed. "We won't be safe until we have it."

I took a step back. "I . . . I don't have it," I stammered.

Mrs. Roland's mouth dropped open. Mr. Roland tensed his shoulders.

"My brother took it," I said. "He took it to Camp Snake Lake with him."

Both parents stared at me, horrified expressions frozen on their faces.

After a few seconds, Mr. Roland spoke in a growl. *"Phears isn't going to like this. We have to go there and get it back!"*

Huh? Did he say *Phears*?

Confused, I took another step back.

Mr. and Mrs. Roland kept their gaze on me. They started to change. Their faces drooped and began to shrink. Their bodies hunched. They curled in on themselves like gloves closing up.

Hard brown shells formed over their clothing. Their heads were small and round now, with tiny black eyes and threadlike tongues lapping the air. They looked like the beetles we studied in science class. Giant growling beetles.

"Oh noooo." A low moan escaped my throat.

They floated off the floor. Floated over me, growling and muttering.

I ducked my head and staggered to the front door. I saw Nicky and Tara, frozen in shock in the middle of the living room.

"Run!" I screamed. "It's a trick. They're not your parents! *Run!*"

But before Nicky and Tara could move, the two giant insects skittered over to them. Grabbed them with their long spindly legs.

They pulled Nicky and Tara against their hard ribbed bodies. Held them tight and started to drag them out the front door.

I staggered to the door. I tried to spin one of the insect creatures around, but my hand slid off its shell.

I grabbed for Tara. Struggling and squirming to free themselves, Nicky and Tara both reached for my outstretched hands.

But the insect creatures wrapped ropelike legs around their middles and held them tight. The giant insects bounced across the front yard like rubber balls, dragging Nicky and Tara with them.

"Let us go! Let us *go*!" Tara wailed.

My heart pounding, I darted over the grass. I could see Mrs. Benson in the window of her house next door. I knew she couldn't see the ghosts. She could only see me. She probably thought I was totally crazy as I went screaming down the lawn and leaped into the air.

I jumped onto the back of one of the enormous insects. I gripped the hard shell with both hands. It felt slick and hot. My hands nearly slipped off.

The ghostly creature had Tara wrapped in its grasp. "Help me, Max!" she screamed. "I . . . I can't get loose!"

With a groan, I lurched backward, trying to pull the insect onto its back.

A puff of black steam shot out from under its shell. I gasped as a putrid smell invaded my nose.

I started to choke and gag. It smelled like day-old vomit. The rank odor surrounded me, clung to my clothes, my hair. I could even taste it on my tongue.

Another strong puff of the disgusting vapor made my stomach heave.

And then the creature twisted its body hard—and sent me flying to the ground. I landed with a heavy thud—and made a grab for one of its wiry legs.

The leg slipped from my hand. Groaning, I jumped to my feet.

"Help—Max!" Nicky screamed.

Holding Nicky tightly, the creature spun around. It stretched out two tendril-like legs and grabbed my head.

The sharp pincers poked through my skin. The legs jerked hard, and I started to spin.

And spin . . .

I couldn't stop twirling.

The trees, the houses, the cars on the street—all spun around me as I twirled, faster and faster.

As I spun, I saw the two insect creatures skittering away with their captives, Nicky and Tara. But I was helpless. No way to save them.

My arms flew wildly in the air as I twirled and twirled.

Dizzy now.

So dizzy. The ground met the sky, and the world became a green and blue blur.

7

So Dizzy . . .

So dizzy, I wanted to fall down. But I couldn't stop twirling.

Then I felt something clamp down on my shoulders. I felt a whoosh of air as I came to a sharp stop.

Something held me tight. I couldn't open my eyes. I knew I'd stopped spinning, but the world still seemed to be shooting around and around me.

Slowly, I opened my eyes. I saw blue sky dotted with puffy white clouds. I saw the grass of the front yard . . . my driveway.

And I looked up at Mrs. Benson, who had clamped her hands onto my shoulders and was gripping me tightly. "Max? What on earth were you doing?" she demanded.

I had to think fast. It wasn't easy. The ground was tilting and the trees were still spinning. "Uh . . . I was practicing for school," I said.

Mrs. Benson squinted at me. "Practicing? Practicing for what?"

"Uh . . . I'm making a top in wood shop," I said. "I was trying to see how it works."

She stared at me some more. Then she finally let go of my shoulders. "Max, you've always been such a weird child," she said.

"Thanks, Mrs. Benson," I replied. I staggered into the house. My legs kept twisting like pretzels. I felt as if my head was spinning on my neck.

I pulled myself up the stairs to my bedroom and dropped down on the edge of my bed.

Now what?

I sat there for a long time, holding my head in my hands and trying to think.

I have to save Nicky and Tara, I decided. The two ghosts were going to Camp Snake Lake to get the pendant. They probably dragged Nicky and Tara with them.

I have to save my friends. And I have to get that pendant away from Colin before those two creatures attack him.

Yes, that's what I have to do.

And how do I do that?

I looked up and saw Mom and Dad at my bedroom door. "I changed my mind," I said, standing up. "I'm going to camp."

A big grin spread over Dad's beefy face. He charged into the room. "That's my man!" he boomed. "I *knew* you weren't a pathetic worm!"

27

He gave me such a hard slap on the back that I went crashing into the wall.

"Thanks, Dad," I said. "Sweet."

"We've got to get you packed right away," Mom said, fluttering around my dresser. "You're going to have such a good time, Max."

Oh, yeah. For sure. Such a good time with a couple of evil ghosts who will do anything—maybe even *kill*—to get that pendant.

Forget about a good time. Is there any way I'll *survive*?

8

THE NEXT MORNING, I helped Mom and Dad load my stuff onto the camp bus, and then I climbed aboard.

"Go get 'em, Tiger!" Dad shouted through the bus window. "Kill 'em at camp! Kill! Kill! Kill!"

Thanks for the great send-off, Dad. And thanks for embarrassing me in front of everyone.

I could feel my face burning. I kept my head down and moved quietly to the back of the bus.

"Kill! Kill! Kill!" a little boy repeated. Everyone laughed.

The bus bounced down our street and turned onto Powell to make more stops. Most of the seats were filled. Kids were talking and joking and laughing. Two boys kept bouncing a rubber ball off a girl's head.

"Stop it!" she cried.

"Make us!" they said.

I slumped low in my seat and stared out the window, thinking hard.

What if the ghosts were already at Camp Snake Lake?

What if my brother tried to keep the pendant, and the ghosts did something *horrible* to him to take it away?

What if the ghosts got the pendant away from Colin—and destroyed Nicky and Tara?

So many questions, all of them terrifying.

The bus jerked to a stop. I saw Traci Wayne climb on. I felt my heart skip a beat.

I don't know if I'm in love with Traci or what. But every time I see her, my ears start to burn, my skin tingles, and I start breathing out of my mouth like this: *whee whee whee,* as if I've just run ten miles.

Traci is blond and beautiful and totally awesome. And she's not stuck up. She just has no time for pond scum like me.

Traci took the empty seat right in front of me. She turned and smiled. "Hi, Max."

Whoa.

Traci Wayne said hi to me!

Normally, I'd do a few somersaults down the bus aisle or maybe sing and dance a jig. But today I was so worried about Nicky and Tara and Colin, I just muttered "Hi" to her. Then I turned back to staring out the window.

The bus rolled along another few blocks, then stopped again. I groaned when I saw who was climbing on this time. The Wilbur brothers—Billy and Willy Wilbur, the worst kids at Jefferson Elementary School.

For some reason, Billy and Willy don't like me. I'm not sure why. Maybe it's because the kids at school all call me Brainimon because I'm the class brain. And these two chimps are still *chewing* on their books.

Luckily, they didn't see me. They took two seats in the middle of the bus, next to a skinny boy with curly blond hair and a face full of freckles.

The bus roared on. Pretty soon we were out on the highway, rolling past farms and empty fields.

The kid next to me—a short pudgy kid in a gray sweatshirt that said I HATE YOU in drippy red letters—had an iPod around his neck and big headphones over his ears. He was snapping his fingers, grooving in his own world.

After a while, I heard the Wilbur brothers talking to the freckle-faced boy next to them. His name was Jakey, and he said he'd never been to camp before and he didn't know what to expect.

Billy Wilbur started telling him about Snake Lake. "It's loaded with poisonous snakes. No lie," Billy said, grinning at his brother.

I heard Jakey gulp.

"Before the end of camp, they make you swim across Snake Lake," Billy said. "Across and back."

"Most kids don't make it all the way," Willy added. "Because snakes wrap around you and cut off your air."

"No way!" Jakey exclaimed in a tiny voice.

Billy lowered his voice to a whisper, but I could still hear him. "When I did it last summer," he said, "a long fat snake curled around my neck. And two snakes curled around my waist."

"And . . . what happened?" Jakey asked.

"I drowned!" Billy replied.

The two Wilburs hee-hawed like donkeys and slapped each other a hard high five.

"You're joking, right?" Jakey said. "You're making it up about the snakes?"

Billy and Willy snickered to each other. "You'll see," Willy said.

I stopped listening to them and stared out the window at the passing trees and fields. I thought hard about Snake Lake. Is it really filled with poisonous snakes? Do we really have to swim in it?

I suddenly felt cold all over. The Wilburs were telling the same story as my brother. It had to be true.

The bus rolled along the highway for another two hours. I spent the time thinking hard about how to get the pendant from Colin and how to rescue Nicky and Tara.

But all my thinking led me nowhere. I didn't have a clue.

The bus pulled off the highway onto a smaller road. We turned at a wooden sign shaped like an arrow that proclaimed CAMP SNAKE LAKE. Then we followed a dirt road through the trees until we came to the camp.

Through the bus window, I saw two rows of small white-shingled cabins. A few larger buildings built of logs. An asphalt basketball court. A tetherball pole.

Behind the cabins, I saw a thin line of trees. And between the trees shimmered the blue water of a lake.

We piled out of the bus onto a gravel path. Billy Wilbur had his hand on Jakey's shoulder. "Watch out for tarantulas in the trees," he whispered to Jakey. "If you see a tree shaking, don't walk under it."

Jakey stared around, his eyes wide. I could see that he was pretty frightened. I shivered too.

A chubby red-faced man came jogging across the grass. His head was shaved bald. He wore a red and white bandanna around his neck. His baggy khaki shorts went down to his knees. His stomach bounced up and down beneath a Camp Snake Lake T-shirt.

"That's Uncle Joey," Billy Wilbur told Jakey. "He owns the camp. If he doesn't like you, he'll send you into the woods at night to look for wolves."

"Wolves?" Jakey squeaked. "There aren't any wolves in these woods—*are* there?"

I saw a bunch of campers run onto the basketball court. Squinting into the sun, I searched for Colin. I knew I had to find him—fast.

"Hey, people—welcome!" Uncle Joey boomed. He wiped his bald head with his bandanna. "Good to see you guys. And welcome to all you new campers."

A group of girls was heading to a set of cabins up on a hill. I guessed that was the girls' camp. I could hear voices from the lake. Were kids swimming there?

No sign of Colin anywhere.

"This is Artie," Uncle Joey said, slapping a young guy on the shoulder. Artie was a short wiry guy with spiky blond hair and a dangling silver earring in one ear. "Artie is the go-to guy at this camp. You got a problem? Go to Artie."

"Hey, dudes, welcome," Artie said, flashing us a double thumbs-up.

"I'm going to take you people to the lodge now," Uncle Joey said. "You'll get your cabin assignments there. And we have camp T-shirts for you. Just tell us your size."

He gazed at Jakey. "I think you'll take an extra small." He chuckled. "Don't worry. We'll pump you up this summer. We'll make a superhero out of you."

34

He squeezed Jakey's skinny arm. "I've seen bigger muscles on a chicken," he said.

Jakey looked really embarrassed. Uncle Joey laughed. He had a deep voice and a booming laugh.

A bunch of crows flew overhead, cawing loudly. I watched them swoop into the woods.

Suddenly, I shivered again. Were the two evil ghosts here already? Had they already found my brother?

"Uncle Joey? Do you know where Colin Doyle is?" I asked.

But he didn't hear me. He and Artie were already jogging over the grass, leading us to the lodge. I was desperate to get to Colin. But I had no choice. I had to stay with the group.

A smiling young woman with blond hair that hung down past her shoulders was waiting for us at a table outside the lodge. She told us her name was Ada and we should come to her if we had any questions. Then she gave us our cabin assignments.

The cabins all had Indian tribe names. Mine was Navajo. And guess who I shared my cabin with? You got it. The Wilbur brothers and Jakey.

Bad news.

As we walked along the dirt path to find Navajo, Jakey broke away from the Wilburs and ran over to me. "Can I have the bunk next to you?" he asked in a tiny voice.

"Yeah, sure. No problem," I said. "Why?"

"Those two brothers are kinda scary," Jakey said.

Tell me about it.

We stepped into the cabin. It was really small. Just enough room for two bunk beds and four little dressers. Where was the bathroom? Outside, at the end of the row of cabins.

Jakey and I claimed the bunks away from the window. He wanted to be against the wall in case a bat swooped in through the open window at night.

Counselors brought our bags and trunks for us to unpack.

A knock on the cabin door made me turn around. Colin strode into the cabin. "You got the crummy cabin," he said, glancing around. "I think some kids died in this cabin. Because of germs and mold in the walls."

I didn't have time for that stupid nonsense. I grabbed Colin by the arm and dragged him outside.

"Listen to me," I said, gripping his arm tightly. "That pendant. I need it. I'm not kidding. I need it back. Please."

Colin pulled his arm away and stepped back. He narrowed his eyes at me. "Are you crazy? That stupid pendant? You'll never find it. I threw it into the woods."

9

"No!" I screamed.

Colin nodded and laughed. "Yes. I didn't like it. I threw it away."

"You're lying!" I cried. "You didn't—*did* you?"

He grinned and danced away from me. "Poor Maxie. You can't cry to Mommy. She isn't here."

"But I need that pendant!" I wailed.

What if Nicky and Tara's parents really were inside it? Did this mean the kids would never see their parents again? All because of stupid Colin?

"Call the other geeks in your cabin," Colin said. "I'm supposed to give them a tour of the camp."

"Call them yourself," I muttered angrily.

He grabbed me by the shoulders. "Hey, I didn't show you the official camp greeting," he said. He made a fist, dug his knuckles into the top of my head, and dragged them back and forth as hard as he could.

"Ow! Stop!" I screamed, trying to escape.

But he scraped his knuckles deeper over my scalp until he had dug a two-inch rut in my head.

When he finally let go, I was howling in pain and holding my throbbing skull with both hands.

"Did that hurt?" Colin asked innocently. "Oops. Sorry." He laughed.

I pressed my head against the cabin wall, waiting for the pain to fade. I heard Colin calling my bunkmates to come out for his camp tour.

We stopped at Arapaho, Iroquois, and Comanche and picked up a bunch of other guys. Traci Wayne and four or five other girls came down from the girls' camp and hung together at the back of the group.

Colin led the way down the path between the rows of cabins. He showed us the main lodge, the theater, the arts and crafts center, and the infirmary. "Sometimes kids who go into the infirmary don't come out," he said, shaking his head.

I heard Jakey gasp.

Colin led us away from the path, into the woods. Butterflies fluttered over a fallen tree trunk. Bright red berries clung to low, prickly shrubs.

We stopped in a small circle of dirt in front of an empty cabin. The shingles on the cabin were rotted and stained. The glass in the windows had been broken out. I saw a wide, jagged hole in the roof tiles.

"This is the abandoned cabin," Colin announced. "Stand back." He pushed a few kids to the edge of the dirt. "The cabin had to be abandoned because it's haunted."

"Yeah, sure," one of Traci's friends muttered.

"Don't ever come here at night," Colin said. "I'm not kidding. It's totally dangerous. A long time ago, some campers died in this cabin. No one knows how. Now they haunt the place. And they hate all campers who are still alive. They want to make you dead like they are. So stay as far away as you can."

I stared at the cabin and suddenly felt a chill. Colin could be telling the truth. The cabin could be haunted.

I gazed through the broken window. Were Nicky and Tara here? Held prisoner by those two ugly insect creatures? This would be the perfect place for them to hide.

Another chill ran down my back.

We turned and started to leave, heading back into the trees—when Colin stopped suddenly. "Hey—" He turned back to the abandoned cabin. "Did you hear anything in there?"

We all froze and listened. I heard Jakey let out a short whimper.

Colin took a few steps back toward the cabin. "I thought I heard something. Like someone moving around inside."

He stepped up to the door. Then he turned

back to us. He waved us back. "Don't move. Stay right there. I'm just going to check it out."

He pushed open the front door and disappeared inside. The door slammed behind him.

We all stood in place watching the cabin. The Wilburs giggled about something and shoved each other. "Let's go," Billy said. "He's never coming back."

Some guys laughed. Jakey moved closer to me. He was biting his bottom lip as he stared at the cabin.

The cabin windows had no glass. But I didn't hear anything from inside. Trees rustled in a warm breeze. The sharp smell of the lake floated over us.

Silence in the cabin.

What was Colin doing? How long would we have to wait?

I stared at the door, waiting for it to open.

We waited some more.

Silence.

"Hey, Colin—what's up?" I shouted. My voice broke. I realized I was totally scared.

No answer to my call.

The Wilburs stopped shoving each other. No one was laughing now. We all stood silently at the edge of the dirt waiting for Colin to come back out.

"Colin—?" I called again.

Finally, the cabin door swung open slowly. I

gasped as a figure came running out—running at us full speed.

Colin?

Oh, *no*!

The front of his T-shirt . . . it was stained with bright red blood. His arms waved frantically in front of him as he bolted toward us. His flip-flops kicked up dirt as he ran.

And above his shirt . . . above his shirt . . .

No head!

No head above the bloodstained T-shirt.

His arms waved wildly. He bolted toward us, staggering as he ran.

And then—from inside the cabin . . . a voice . . . a *screaming* voice from the open cabin windows.

Colin's voice!

"Help me! My body! Where is my body?"

10

I LET OUT A CRY. Beside me, Jakey opened his mouth in a scream.

Traci pressed her hands to her cheeks. The Wilbur brothers staggered back, mouths open.

"Where is my body?"

The voice inside the cabin was my brother's. And here was his headless body, lurching toward us.

"Noooo!" I wailed as he crashed into me. The sticky, bloodstained T-shirt swiped my face. The two of us tumbled to the ground.

I thrashed and kicked and shoved his body off me. Then I leaped to my feet.

A head poked out from inside the T-shirt. *Not* my brother's head! Another boy, dark-haired, brown-eyed, laughing hard.

His T-shirt had been pulled up high to hide his head.

My heart pounding, I turned and saw my brother step out of the cabin. "My body!" he shouted. "Where's my body?"

And then, laughing and hooting, he and the other boy slapped each other high and low fives and shoved each other and acted like total goofs. They were so happy with the joke they had pulled on us.

"Very funny," I told my brother. "Remind me to laugh later."

Billy Wilbur had a big grin on his face. "They played that same joke last year. But Willy and I kept quiet about it."

"We didn't want to spoil the fun," Willy said.

"Just a way of warning you guys to stay away from the haunted cabin," Colin said.

"Catch you later, dude," the other boy said. He trotted off.

"Good work, Chris!" Colin called after him.

"Let's go. One more stop, guys," Colin said. He led the way down a path through the woods. "Next is the scariest place of all."

I held back. I turned and gazed at the abandoned cabin one more time. A light breeze rattled the loose shutters. And over the clattering, I heard a whisper. . . .

"Max . . . Max . . ."

My breath caught in my throat. Someone whispering my name? Calling to me?

"Max . . ."

Nicky and Tara held prisoner inside there, calling for help?

43

A cold sweat broke out on my face. I took a step toward the cabin. Then another. The sun faded behind a cloud, and a dark shadow washed over the cabin.

"Max . . ." The whisper in the wind. I wasn't imagining it.

Were my two ghost friends in there? If they were, I had to rescue them.

My legs trembled as I made my way into the deep shadow around the cabin. I was only a few feet from the door when a shout broke the silence:

"Max! Get over here!"

11

I SPUN AND SAW COLIN. He stood with his hands cupped around his mouth. He shouted again. "Jerk Face, get over here! Keep up with the tour!"

"But—" I hesitated. The sun beamed down again, sweeping the shadow away. The cabin stood in silence now.

"Hurry up!" Colin shouted.

With a sigh, I jogged across the grass. As I passed him, Colin gave me a hard slap on the back. "Owww!" I knew my back would stop stinging in a day or two.

We followed Colin through the trees to the lake. I saw Traci catch a butterfly in her hands. The other girls oohed and aahed.

Jakey walked close beside me. He had beads of sweat on his forehead. The Headless Camper routine had really frightened us both.

"Why are they always trying to scare us here?" he asked. "We came to camp to have fun."

"Beats me," I muttered.

I was still thinking about the abandoned cabin.

I kept turning back, expecting the two evil creatures to come scrambling after us and grab Colin.

They think he has the pendant. What will they do to him when he tells them he tossed it into the woods?

Colin could end up as the Headless Camper after all!

I wanted to save my brother—but how? If I explained the whole thing to him, he'd laugh at me. He'd tell me to quit making up dumb ghost stories.

Then he'd probably hit me so hard I'd stop breathing for an hour or two. And he'd tell me it was for my own good.

So—no way to talk to Colin.

Maybe the only way to save his life was to find the pendant. But how could I do that?

We waded through tall grass and came to the lakeshore. My sneakers sank into the soft mud. The water rippled gently, flat and blue under the clear blue sky.

Far to our left, two silvery canoes bobbed in the water, tied to a short wooden pier.

Shielding my eyes from the bright sun, I gazed out over the lake. I heard frogs croaking and birds chirping in the trees behind the lake.

"Welcome to Snake Lake, guys," Colin said. "Awesome-looking, huh?"

We mumbled a reply.

A kid picked up a small stone and made it skip over the water.

"Hey! Don't disturb the snakes," Colin warned. "This lake is filled with poisonous snakes. Big ones. They've killed most of the fish. And now they're always hungry."

My heart started to thud in my chest.

Behind me, a couple of kids snickered.

"This is no joke," Colin said. "We don't swim in this lake. And I'm not making this up. You put one foot in Snake Lake and the snakes come swimming for you instantly."

He pulled off his flip-flops and took a few steps into the water. "Here. Let me show you," he said.

We watched as he stood perfectly still, water up over his ankles. A few seconds went by. Then I thought I saw ripples in the water.

"*Owwww!*" Colin let out a scream. He jerked his bare foot out of the water. Staggering on one leg, he frantically rubbed the foot. "*Owwww.* They *got* me! It *hurts!*"

A few kids gasped. Others grew silent. The Wilburs laughed.

Colin stepped out of the water and bent to put on his flip-flops. "Okay, that was a joke," he said. "But everything I said about Snake Lake is true. You cannot swim here because the snakes own the place. No lie."

"Then where do we swim?" a boy asked.

Colin pointed behind us. "In the smaller lake by the girls' cabins. Be very careful around here, guys. I'm totally serious. Most of these snakes are deadly. If you get bitten, you die in thirty seconds."

Colin brushed his blond hair off his forehead. "That's the tour, dudes," he said. "Now here's a little test for you guys. Let's see if you can get back to your cabins without me."

He turned and took off, running through the tall grass toward the trees. We stood and watched him.

When he reached the trees, he turned back. "Hey, Maxie!" he shouted. "Maxie, check this out!"

He reached under his T-shirt, struggled with something—pulled it out and held it up.

The pendant!

"See ya, dude!" he called, laughing. Then he disappeared into the trees.

12

COLIN HAD LIED. He still had the pendant. Was that good news or bad?

I didn't have time to think about it. I heard shouts behind me.

I turned and saw the Wilbur brothers grab Jakey. He squirmed and struggled. But they lifted him off the ground and raised him to their shoulders.

"Let me go! Let me go!" Jakey was squawking like a chicken.

Everyone else just stood and stared as the Wilburs carried Jakey like a canoe to the water. "Let's test the water!" Billy exclaimed.

"Let me go! Please! Stop it! Stop!"

"Nice day for a swim, hey, Jakey?" Willy said.

"No! I don't want to! I don't want to!"

The Wilburs were too strong for Jakey. No way could he squirm free. They lifted him high over their heads and stepped up to the edge of the water.

"No! Don't!" I heard Traci scream.

49

Willy Wilbur tossed back his head and laughed.

"Hey, snakes! Here comes lunch!" Billy shouted. He and his brother raised Jakey higher and prepared to heave him into the water.

Jakey was pleading and wailing.

"Calling all snakes! Wake up!" Billy shouted. "Here comes some fresh meat!"

"Let Jakey go!" I shouted. I took a deep breath and ran to rescue the poor kid.

My sneakers sank into the soft mud on the shore. And then I took a wild leap at Jakey.

The Wilburs jerked him to one side—and I flew past them. And sailed headfirst into the water.

I sank to the bottom, my clothes and sneakers helping to pull me down. I must have been in two or three feet of water. But the shock of the cold paralyzed me for a moment.

I stretched out my hands and kicked my feet and started to float.

Then I felt the first tickle on my face.

And then another.

Something brushed my cheek and slid past my ear.

Something tickled the back of my neck.

Something wrapped itself around my arm.

The snakes.

The snakes were real—and they were about to start eating their lunch.

13

PANIC FROZE MY MUSCLES. I couldn't move.

A snake slithered across my neck. Another one curled over my ear.

I jerked alert. Kicked my legs hard—and felt the soft, muddy bottom.

Tearing at the snakes, slapping them off my face, I scrambled to my feet. I sucked in breath after breath of air.

Trembling, I pulled a snake off my chest. And another one from my hair. "S-snakes!" I choked out. "They're . . . all over me."

I saw the kids laughing at me. It took me a few seconds to understand why.

The snakes on my body—they weren't snakes. They were lake grass. Long, wet blades of grass.

I shuddered, struggling to catch my breath.

The Wilbur brothers let Jakey go. He ran behind the group of kids, *way* behind them. He was hugging himself, a frightened expression on his face.

The others laughed at me.

"Okay, okay," I muttered. "It was only weeds or something."

I stomped away from the shore. My T-shirt and shorts were soaked, and I couldn't stop shivering.

"Hey, Max?" Someone was calling me. I turned to see Traci running across the grass toward me.

I pulled another long blade of grass off the back of my neck. At the edge of the water, the other kids were still laughing. One of them started to imitate me, slapping at his face and body, pretending to pull snakes off.

"Big joke," I muttered, avoiding Traci's eyes.

"Well, I thought you were totally brave," Traci said.

"Huh?" I turned to her. "Really?"

"Trying to save that little guy was awesome," Traci said. Her smile made me feel warm all over. The sunlight reflected off her beautiful blond hair.

"Of course, falling headfirst in the lake made you look like a total klutz," she added. Then she went running back to her friends.

I just stood there with my mouth open. Traci Wayne had paid me a compliment!

Traci Wayne had said something nice to me!

I couldn't get to sleep that night. I kept thinking about Nicky and Tara and remembering those two evil creatures who had dragged them away.

And I kept thinking about the life pod. How could we find out whether Nicky and Tara's parents were inside the pod if we couldn't get it away from my stupid brother?

It was a hot, damp night. I kicked off my blanket and tossed and turned on my bunk. Sweat prickled the back of my neck.

Finally, I dropped to the floor, pulled on shorts and a T-shirt, and crept outside for some fresh air. A tiny sliver of a moon greeted me overhead. It looked like a cat's grin. The sky was filled with stars.

I took a deep breath and started walking along the path to the woods. Crickets chirped all around me, and the trees made a whispering sound.

I stopped walking when I heard voices. Shouts and laughter. They seemed to be coming from the lake.

I turned into the woods and followed the path to the lakeshore. The voices grew louder. I recognized Colin's voice. He was shouting about how cold the water was.

Through the trees, I could see a bunch of kids swimming and splashing in the lake. Counselors and junior counselors were having a late-night swim.

Swimming in Snake Lake.

So the stories about the lake *weren't* true. The lake *wasn't* filled with poisonous snakes. It was just one more story to frighten the new campers.

Okay. No big surprise there.

I didn't really care about that. All I cared about was finding the pendant.

I squinted hard and spotted Colin. He was having a splashing war with two of the girl counselors.

I can search his cabin, I thought. Colin bunked with four other junior counselors in a cabin near the lodge. They were all in the lake. The cabin would be empty . . .

. . . and maybe Colin had left the pendant there before he went for his swim.

I didn't walk to Colin's cabin. I ran.

My flip-flops slapped along the dirt path. I was breathing hard by the time I reached the cabin. It was dark inside. I knocked on the door, softly at first, then a little more loudly.

The crickets stopped chirping. Silence now.

Something low and small scampered away from the cabin wall. A fox. The camp was overrun by foxes, which came out of the woods at night searching for food.

I watched it slink away. Then I knocked one more time on the cabin door. No answer. The cabin was empty.

Was the pendant there?

I pulled open the door and slipped inside.

14

BLINKING IN THE DARKNESS, I bumped my knee on the first bunk. Pain shot up my leg. I rubbed my knee, waiting for it to stop throbbing. Then I found a flashlight hanging by the cabin door.

I swept the light around the cabin. I moved it from bunk to bunk to make sure no one was there.

I spotted Colin's shirt on a lower bunk against the wall. Keeping the light on the bed, I crossed the room to investigate.

He had left a pile of stuff next to the balled-up shirt. I saw his wallet, some keys, some change. I picked up the shirt and looked underneath.

No. No pendant.

I pulled up the bedsheet and blanket and searched under the pillow. The light trembled in my hand.

Please, let it be here. Please, let me find it.

I moved to the chest of drawers next to the bunk bed. I swept the flashlight over it and saw a stack of magazines and a box of tissues on the dresser.

Which drawer was Colin's?

I pulled open the top drawer. It was stuffed with underwear and socks and swim trunks. The second drawer had Colin's CD player in it and a bunch of CDs. I bent down to open the bottom drawer.

Empty.

Where else could I look?

I dropped to my knees and shone the light under the bed. Colin had shoved his suitcase under there.

He wouldn't put the pendant in his suitcase, I decided.

It's not here. He must be wearing it. He doesn't want me to get it, so he wears it wherever he goes.

I let out a sigh. This was a total waste of time.

Beads of sweat rolled down my forehead. With a groan, I climbed to my feet.

Then I felt a hard tap on my shoulder and I screamed.

15

STARTLED, I DROPPED to the floor. I turned and shone the light on the figure behind me.

"Jakey? What are *you* doing here?" I choked out.

"I woke up and saw you were gone," Jakey said. "Then I saw the light in this cabin. What's up, Max?"

"Huh? What's up with *you*?" I demanded. "Are you following me?"

"No way," he replied. He helped pull me to my feet. "I'm kinda scared," he said. "The Wilbur brothers say they're going to take me out to the woods tomorrow and tie me to a tree."

"I don't think so," I said. "I'll protect you from those geeks, Jakey."

"They're in my face because I'm little and because it's my first time at camp," Jakey said.

"I'll watch out for you," I said. "No problem."

I swept the light one more time over Colin's

57

bed. But no. The pendant didn't magically appear.

Then I put my hand on Jakey's shoulder and led him out of the cabin. Of course, I had no way of knowing the terrifying trouble Jakey would cause for me the next day.

16

I **LOOKED FOR COLIN** at breakfast, but he wasn't at the junior counselors' table. I ran over to Artie, who was pouring orange juice from a big pitcher. "Have you seen my brother?" I asked.

Artie set down the pitcher. "Colin? He went on a canoe trip."

My mouth dropped open. "He already left? For how long?"

Artie shrugged. "Two days, I think. He took some guys with him. He left at dawn." He squinted at me. "You need something?"

Yeah. I need the pendant around his neck.

"No. Guess not," I said.

Would those evil insect creatures follow Colin for the pendant? Would Colin ever return?

I slunk back to the table. I felt sick. I couldn't eat the watery scrambled eggs or the soggy hash browns.

The guys at my table were talking and laughing. But I didn't hear them. I couldn't think of anything but ghosts and that pendant.

Uncle Joey stood in front of the big stone fireplace and announced the morning's activity—a three-mile hike through the woods.

Some kids groaned.

That made Uncle Joey unhappy. "Bad attitude," he said. "That's not the Snake Lake way! Come on, people. Let's hear the Snake Lake fight song!"

We all began to hiss like snakes. The hissing grew louder and echoed off the low redwood ceiling beams of the mess hall.

"That's what we want to hear!" Uncle Joey exclaimed. "Let's hear it again!"

We all hissed again.

"Stop spitting on me!" Jakey cried. He was sitting next to Billy Wilbur. And Billy was deliberately spitting into Jakey's face as he hissed.

Willy started spitting too. And then a couple of other guys decided to try it. And in seconds, there was a spitting war with everyone hissing and spitting.

Spit flew like a rainstorm—until Uncle Joey waved his hands frantically above his head and shouted for silence.

"We're mean as snakes—remember that!" Uncle Joey shouted. "That's the Snake Lake tradition, guys!"

Jakey was wiping spit from his hair and off his cheeks.

"Artie will meet you at nine-thirty in front of the lodge," Uncle Joey announced. "Wear your hiking shoes. You're going up some steep hills."

"Go, Snakes, go!" Artie shouted, slapping high fives as we left the mess hall. He was a gung ho kind of guy.

He never walked. He always ran. And he was always clapping his hands and cheering guys on.

Artie wore sleeveless white T-shirts, and he had big red and blue tattoos of eagles on both arms.

How old was Artie? I wondered. Sixteen or seventeen? And his parents let him get those tattoos?

Weird.

Back in my cabin, I changed into my sneakers and jeans. I rubbed sunscreen all over. Then I stuck a bottle of water in my backpack.

Across the cabin, Willy and Billy were talking to Jakey. "When we get to the top, you have to leap over Howler's Gorge," Willy said. "It's a pretty far jump, Jakey—especially for a little guy like you."

"And if you don't make it, you fall straight down. Into a pit of quicksand," Billy said.

"Yeah, last year a kid didn't make it. He dropped like a rock to the bottom," Willy added.

"They pulled him out of the quicksand, but it wasn't easy," Billy said. "It was already up to his neck. And it was so burning hot, it turned his whole body purple."

"And it stayed purple till the end of camp," his brother said.

Jakey turned to me. "They're lying, right?"

I shrugged. "I don't know."

The Wilburs tossed back their heads and laughed. "You'll see."

"Why do they call it Howler's Gorge?" Jakey asked in a tiny voice.

"Because when you fall, you howl all the way down," Billy said. He clapped Jakey on the back. "You'll see."

And for once, the Wilbur brothers weren't lying.

17

IT WAS A LONG HIKE, but it wasn't bad. If you like a lot of trees, and shrubs, and grassy hills, and chickadees chirping, and hawks and crows and other birds swooping overhead.

Not my thing, really. Exercise always gives me hiccups.

It got really hot as we followed Artie up the hills. My T-shirt stuck to my back, and I had to keep wiping sweat off my face. I finished my bottle of water halfway up the first hill.

Artie kept making us sing songs and do the Snake Lake battle cry. He jogged up the hills, clapping his hands and shouting. Wow. He was like a gung ho *machine*.

There were about thirty of us, mostly guys. But Traci Wayne and four of her friends had some free time, so they tagged along.

I think Traci smiled at me once. But she may have been smiling at someone else.

Jakey and I walked at the back of the group. I tried to push low tree branches out of his way.

And I helped tug him up the steep parts of the climb.

The Wilbur brothers kept swinging on tree limbs and throwing stones down the hills, shouting and hooting and doing cartwheels. They were trying to impress the girls. I was glad the two pests were leaving Jakey and me alone.

Breathing hard, my legs aching, I followed the others up a steep hill covered in tall grass. And at the top stood Howler's Gorge.

Believe it or not, it was just as the Wilburs had described it.

The ground flattened out at the top of the hill and ended in a steep cliff. The other side was four or five feet away.

Jakey and I walked up to the edge and peered down the cliff. We were looking at a long, straight drop to the bottom.

Was it burning-hot quicksand down there? I didn't want to know.

"This is an easy jump, guys," Artie shouted. "No one has ever had any trouble with it. You just have to get a good running start. Watch me."

Artie backed up a few feet, lowered his head as he started to run—and leaped easily over the gorge. Then he leaped back. Then he leaped across one more time. And leaped back.

"See? Easy," he said. "I'm not even out of

breath." He clapped his hands. "Let's go, guys! Let's do it the Snake Lake way!"

Jakey and I stood far back from the gorge. Jakey chewed his bottom lip and kept tugging at his hair. I could see he was tense about it.

But everyone made the jump with no problem. The Wilburs went first. They jumped together, waving their arms above their heads and shrieking as if they were on a roller coaster.

Traci flew high over the gorge, her blond hair waving behind her. She landed gracefully with plenty of room to spare. She clapped for her friends as they jumped easily too.

Jakey and I moved closer and closer to the gorge. "Is there a taxi I can take from here?" I asked.

I was trying to lighten things up. But Jakey didn't crack a smile.

I tried again. "Anyone got a ladder?"

"Your turn," Artie called to Jakey. He patted Jakey on the back. "Let's see what you've got, dude."

Jakey had a wild look on his face. He stared down to the bottom of the gorge. He made a loud gulping sound.

"Fly, man!" Artie exclaimed.

Jakey took a few steps back. He glanced at me. I flashed him a thumbs-up.

He scraped his sneakers back and forth in the dirt. Then he leaned forward—and took off.

He was almost to the cliff edge when he slipped. His feet flew out from under him—and he fell headfirst. Headfirst over the edge.

"Ohhh!" I let out a cry as Jakey started to slide down.

Artie stared openmouthed, frozen in shock.

I had to grab Jakey before he fell. I had to grab his legs before he slid over the side.

I lunged forward. Leaped into the air to make a flying tackle.

Leaped too far!

And went sailing over the edge, into the gorge.

18

IT SEEMED TO HAPPEN in slow motion.

I felt a whoosh of warm air as I started to plunge down the narrow canyon. My hair blew back. No time to shut my eyes.

The sides of the cliffs whirred past, a blur of brown and green. The dark floor of the gorge appeared to rise to meet me.

The wind pushed against my face, my body, as if trying to send me back to the top.

But no. I was falling, sailing down head-first.

Finally, I shut my eyes. And waited for the crushing pain.

Waited . . .

And felt strong hands grip my arms.

In midair?

I opened my eyes—and saw Nicky and Tara. They floated at my sides. They both gripped me under the arms and held tight.

I was too frightened to make a sound.

I felt a strong rush of air against my body as I

stopped falling. I hung upside down, the canyon floor not far below me.

Nicky and Tara held on to me until my legs dropped beneath me and I was right side up. Then they floated up, carrying me with them. And they dropped me back on solid ground.

Dazed and dizzy, I shook my head hard. I still had the roar of the wind in my ears. It took me a while to realize that everyone was clapping and cheering.

Jakey clapped the loudest. His cheek was scratched where he had scraped it against a rock. Otherwise he was fine. He had caught himself in time.

Artie put his hand on my trembling shoulder. He brought his face close to mine and studied me. "How did you do that, dude?" he asked.

"Uh . . . my dad got me flying lessons," I said.

Artie stared hard at me, scratching his head.

After I'd caught my breath, I jumped over the gorge. Kids pounded me on the back and slapped me high fives. Even the Wilbur brothers congratulated me for my awesome feat. And Traci flashed me a big smile.

Jakey made the jump. Artie followed him. And we were all on the other side of the gorge.

I glanced around for Nicky and Tara. Where

were they? How did they escape from those two evil insect creatures?

I let out a happy cry when I saw my two friends floating next to Traci. "There you are!" I cried, running over.

Traci squinted at me. "Where else would I be?"

"Thanks for saving me," I told Nicky and Tara.

"Huh? I didn't do anything, Max!" Traci said, taking a step back.

I gave Nicky and Tara a thumbs-up. "That was good timing," I said.

"Max, did you land on your head down there?" Traci asked.

"I'm not talking to you," I told her.

Traci glanced around. "I'm the only one here."

"We can't talk now," Tara said.

"We *have* to talk," I told Tara.

"Excuse me? Talk? Talk about what?" Traci asked.

"Meet me later," I said to the two ghosts.

"No way!" Traci cried. She made a disgusted face and stomped away. "Artie," she called. "You'd better check out Max. I think he's gone psycho."

"Okay, guys," Artie called. "Let's all jump back over the gorge and head back to camp!"

19

LATE THAT NIGHT, I waited till everyone in my cabin was asleep. I grabbed a can of bug repellent off the dresser and sneaked outside to meet Nicky and Tara. As I sprayed myself with the bug spray, Nicky and Tara floated beside me.

"I'm so glad to see you!" I cried.

Nicky frowned at me. "Max, next time you take a dive, make sure there's water in the pool."

Tara slid her arm around my shoulders. "Where would you be without us, Max?"

"Where have you been?" I cried. "I—I've been looking for you for days."

"We just escaped," Tara said. "We . . . we were so scared."

"We're still scared," Nicky said. "Those two creatures who pretended to be our parents? They're still here. Hiding in that abandoned cabin in the woods."

"And so is Phears," Tara added.

I let out a cry. Huh? Phears? Oh no. Oh wow.

I knew Phears. I knew he was the most frightening ghost of them all. He called himself the Animal Traveler. He hid inside animals. Then he blew the animals apart and came sailing out.

Phears has terrifying powers. His hobby is hurting people. He once pulled back my dog's skin and turned him completely inside out. Then he started to do the same thing to me.

"He's here. We saw him," Tara said. She chewed her bottom lip.

"The two insects dragged us to camp. They really want that pendant," Nicky whispered.

"Our parents *have* to be inside it," Tara said. "Why else would they be so desperate to get their hands on it?"

"The insects hid in the empty cabin. They planned to go after your brother. But Phears appeared," Nicky said. "Guess what? He's their leader. They work for him."

"Phears has been here all along," Tara said, glancing around the dark camp. "He's been watching you, Max."

I swallowed. The night suddenly grew a lot colder.

"Phears got in a big argument with the two ghosts," Nicky said. "He was furious because it was taking them so long to get the pendant. He called them all kinds of names. They started shoving each other. It turned into a real fight."

"That's how we escaped," Tara said. "Nicky

and I slipped away while they were fighting. They didn't even see us go."

"But we know what their plan is," Nicky said, lowering his voice. "They're waiting for *you* to do the work, Max. They're waiting for you to get the pendant. Then they're going to pounce."

I gulped. "Pounce?"

Tara nodded. "They're here. They're watching. They're ready to pounce."

And then I heard a cracking sound behind me.

I spun around. And cried out, "Phears!"

20

NICKY GRABBED ME. "Shhh. Max, don't lose it. That was a tree branch creaking."

My heart had leaped to my throat. I blinked several times, then glanced down the long row of cabins, all dark and silent.

"We have to get out of here!" I cried. "I can't face Phears again!"

"We can't leave," Tara said. "We have to find that pendant. We have to find Mom and Dad. They are so close. I know they are."

"Where is Colin?" Nicky asked me. "Maybe Tara and I can slip into his cabin and take the pendant away from him while he sleeps."

I shook my head. "He isn't here. He went on a two-day canoe trip with some kids."

"Was he wearing the pendant?" Tara asked.

"I don't know. He keeps teasing me with it. Pulling it out from under his shirt and showing it off to me. It doesn't belong to him. He's a total thief."

"Thief?" a voice cried.

I turned and saw Uncle Joey standing beside me. "Who is a thief, Max?" he demanded. "Who are you talking to?"

Tara poked me in the side. "Tell him to mind his own business, Max."

"I can't say that!" I told her.

Uncle Joey squinted at me. "You can't tell me who you were talking to? Was it a girl? Did you sneak out to meet a girl?"

"Is there room for us in your cabin?" Nicky asked me. "Do you have a lot of other guys in there?"

"No. Three," I said.

Uncle Joey's eyes bulged. "You sneaked out to meet *three* girls?"

"I wasn't talking to you," I said.

Uncle Joey studied me. "Max, did you hit your head when you fell down the gorge?"

Tara grabbed my arm. "Max, tell him to go away. We have to talk."

"No," I said. "Shut up."

Uncle Joey's face twisted into an angry scowl. "You're telling me to shut up? Would you like to be on latrine duty and mop up the bathrooms for a week?"

"Tell him to get lost!" Tara said.

"Make me!" I cried.

Uncle Joey shrugged. "Okay, I will. You're on latrine duty for a week, Max."

I turned angrily to Tara. "Thanks a lot!" I shouted.

"You're welcome," Uncle Joey said. "Now get back to your cabin." He crossed his arms and glared at me.

I had no choice. I had a hundred things I wanted to ask Nicky and Tara. But with Uncle Joey watching, I turned and trudged up the path to the cabins.

Owls hooted in the trees. A strong breeze off the lake made the trees creak and shiver. Flying low overhead, a bat fluttered back and forth across the path.

I was almost to my cabin when I heard the whispers.

"Max . . . Maaaaaax . . ."

Again. Someone whispering my name. From the empty cabin in the woods. The Haunted Cabin.

"Maaaaaaaax . . ."

No. Not from the cabin. Too close.

Right behind me!

I spun around—and stared at the two insect creatures.

Taller than me, standing on their back legs. Buzzing excitedly. Whispering, *"Maaaax . . . Maaaax . . ."*

Their tiny black eyes glowed in the moonlight. Their antennae rattled over their heads.

75

I let out a loud gasp and tried to run.

But they were too fast for me. One scrabbled in front of me, and I stumbled into it. Its ribbed chest felt hard as iron.

The other one bumped me from behind.

"Maaax. Maaax." A raspy, metallic sound.

"Too slow, Max. You're too slow."

"We need the pendant now. We warned you."

"Too slow."

"And now it's too late."

With loud grunts, they shoved their hard ribbed bodies against me. One from in front, the other from behind.

Pain jolted my body.

They're crushing me, I realized.

They're not going to wait for Colin.

They're crushing me right now.

21

MY CHEST ACHED. I couldn't breathe.

I felt the warm vibrations of their chests as they tightened themselves against me, pressing harder, smothering me against their insect bodies.

Then I heard a loud *crack*.

My bones breaking!

But no. I heard a soft explosion. And then a powerful stinging odor spread over me.

It took me a second to realize what it was. The can of bug spray. Crushed between the two creatures, the can had exploded.

The stinging mist floated up around us.

I heard the creatures sigh.

Their chests went soft. I could feel the ribbed flesh collapsing.

They toppled off me and began to stagger crazily, coughing and sputtering. Their antennae drooped. The glow faded from their tiny round eyes. They grabbed at their chests, wheezing, heads tossed back, roaring hoarsely like elephants.

And then they collapsed. Their bodies made a wet smacking sound as they hit the muddy ground. Their heads slid into their shells. Their spindly legs curled into their chests.

They didn't move.

Dead. The two creatures were dead.

I stood over them, still panting. I pressed my hands to my knees and struggled to catch my breath.

The two insect creatures were dead. But I knew I couldn't celebrate. I knew Phears was still around.

Waiting to pounce.

Phears would be angry now. Phears would be coming after me soon.

And I knew it would take more than a can of bug spray to get rid of him.

22

AFTER KILLING TWO DANGEROUS CREATURES, mopping the latrines wasn't that difficult. In fact, it helped take my mind off my troubles. I held the mop in one hand and pinched my nose with two fingers of my other hand. No problem.

I mopped all six latrines after breakfast, and it only took an hour. While I worked, I made up word games in my head.

Did you know that an anagram for CAMP SNAKE LAKE is SNEAK LAME PACK?

I know. It doesn't make any sense. But what do you expect from someone cleaning toilets?

I did the word games to keep my mind off Colin and the pendant and Phears. Artie told me that Colin was supposed to return from his canoe trip later that afternoon.

It was a chilly gray day. Dark storm clouds gathered overhead. In the woods, a white blanket of fog rolled along the ground.

Right after lunch, the rain started to come

down. Thunder cracked overhead. We all gathered in the lodge.

Uncle Joey showed a movie on the big-screen TV. It was a Jackie Chan film, very funny with lots of kicking and guys flying through the air.

The girls groaned and complained about how stupid and violent it was. But the guys liked it.

Some kids sat cross-legged on the floor. Some sprawled on their backs and used other kids for pillows.

The rain pattered down on the roof of the lodge, making it hard to hear the movie. I couldn't concentrate on it anyway. I knew Colin would be back in camp any minute.

About halfway through the film, I sneaked out the back door. I stood outside the lodge and let the rain pour over me. It was almost as dark as night. I squinted into the eerie gray light, watching for my brother.

To my right, the pounding rain had turned the dirt path to the cabins into a river. To my left, the lake stretched dark and still. Raindrops sparkled like little diamonds as they hit the surface.

Thunder rumbled, far in the distance now. And I saw a pale streak of lightning high in the gray-purple sky.

I sighed. I could be home safe and sound in my

room. Instead, here I was somewhere far out in the woods, surrounded by ghosts.

And just as I thought about ghosts, Nicky and Tara appeared in front of me. I watched the raindrops fall right through them and hit the ground at their feet.

They were standing in the rain, but they weren't getting wet.

"What's up, Max?" Tara asked.

"Is Colin back?" Nicky asked.

I opened my mouth to answer them but stopped. A figure moved down by the lake. A chill swept down my back. Phears?

No. I recognized Colin. Colin back from his trip, dragging a canoe, holding it upside down over his head as an umbrella. He was moving slowly, like some kind of lumbering animal.

"Th-there he is," I said, pointing.

"Let me handle this," Tara said, blocking my path.

"Handle it?" I asked. "What do you mean?"

"He can't see me, right? I can just pull open his shirt and remove the pendant before he knows what's happening," Tara said.

"But—but he's really strong. He'll fight you," I said.

"I'll go with you," Nicky said. "I'll hold Colin's arms behind him while you get the pendant off."

"Let me help," I said.

Tara pushed me back. "It's *our* mom and dad inside the pendant," she said. "Let *us* rescue them, Max."

Nicky and Tara became invisible.

The wind shifted, splashing cold rain in my face. Wiping it away, I watched my brother move slowly across the lakeshore. And I crossed my fingers.

23

THE RAIN POUNDED down hard. Colin trudged along the shore, holding the aluminum canoe over his head. Suddenly, the canoe rose into the air.

Colin let out a startled cry. He gripped the sides of the canoe. I knew Nicky and Tara were trying to pull it away from him. I watched my startled brother struggle to hold on.

"Stupid wind!" Colin shouted.

Did he really believe it was the wind?

Finally, the canoe appeared to sail away from him. It landed upside down on the ground. Colin stared down at it, looking confused.

Colin's hands suddenly flew behind his back. His eyes bulged. "Hey—!" he cried out. "Let go! Who's there?"

He was wearing a long-sleeved plaid shirt over a T-shirt. I watched the buttons start to come undone, one by one from the top down.

Hurry, Tara, I thought.

Colin stared down goggle-eyed as his shirt

appeared to unbutton itself. He squirmed and struggled. But he couldn't free his arms.

The third button came undone—and Colin's shirt flew open, flapping in the wind.

Colin let out a frightened shriek. *Now* he knew it wasn't the wind! The wind doesn't unbutton your shirt!

He squirmed and ducked and tried to twist free of whatever was holding him. "Who's there?" he screamed again. "I can't see you! Let me go!"

I loved watching him squirm. He always made fun of my ghost stories. Maybe he'd believe me the next time I told him I was haunted!

Suddenly, Colin dropped onto his back and started to kick his feet. "Stop it! Stop it!" he shouted, wriggling like a worm. "I'm *ticklish*!"

His open shirt flapped in the wind. "Max! Max!" Tara's shout rang out over the roar of the wind.

"Tara—what's wrong?" I called.

"It isn't here!" she screamed. "He isn't wearing it!"

24

"**Noooooo!**" I opened my mouth in a furious cry.

He stole that pendant from me, I thought, and we really need it.

A wave of anger swept over me.

That big jerk can't keep it from us!

I took off, running across the rain-soaked grass. My sneakers splashed up waves of water as I ran.

"Colin!" I shouted. "Colin! Colin!" I just kept shouting his name.

He jumped to his feet, his eyes wide with surprise. "Max? What are you doing out here? What's your problem?"

I lowered my head and ran right into him. I wrapped my arms around his knees and tackled him to the ground.

We both landed hard. "Way to go, Max!" I heard Nicky shout.

"Give me my pendant!" I screamed in a high, hoarse voice. "Give it to me! Give it to me!"

I climbed on top of Colin and sat on his chest. He lay on his back, gasping in shock.

He'd never seen me lose it like this before. After all, he was the big tough dude and I was the weak geeky shrimp.

Only this time, I really wanted something. I was going to get that pendant back no matter what Colin did.

"Give it to me! Give it!" I started pounding his chest with my fists. "Give it!"

"Okay, okay." Colin raised both hands in surrender. "Okay. No problem, Maxie. You can have your stupid, babyish pendant back."

"Really?" I said, breathing hard.

"Just get off me, man. I'll give it to you. Promise."

"No tricks?" I said.

"No tricks."

Slowly, I climbed off his chest and stood up. My legs were shaky. My heart pounded in my chest. We were both drenched.

I knew Nicky and Tara were watching. But they were still invisible.

Colin kept his eyes narrowed at me. I think he was still in shock because little Maxie overpowered him like that.

So was I!

I pushed my wet hair out of my eyes. "Where is it?" I asked Colin. "Do you have it?"

He nodded. "Yeah. I have it. Why is it so important?"

"It's mine," I said. "That's all."

"It's definitely not around his neck," Tara said. "He might be lying."

"Where is it, Colin?" I demanded, holding out my hand for it. "Come on. Give."

"Okay, okay," he said. "You really are a weird little creep, Max."

"Save the compliments, okay?" I said.

"And of course I'm going to pound you to sawdust later. You're sawdust. You realize that, right, man?"

I nodded. "Yeah. Right. I'm sawdust. Give it, Colin."

He reached into his jeans pocket and . . . pulled out the pendant.

Yesssss! He had it!

He held it high above my head. "You want it, Maxie? You want the pendant so badly? Well . . . you can have it. Go chase it!"

He pulled back his arm—and flung the pendant far out into Snake Lake.

25

I WATCHED IT DROP into the water. It made a little splash, bobbed on the surface for about five seconds, then sank out of sight.

"Ohhhhh." A low moan escaped my open mouth.

Colin ran off, laughing at the top of his lungs.

Nicky and Tara appeared. They didn't look happy.

Tara turned away so I wouldn't see the tears in her eyes. Nicky stared down at the muddy ground, his hands shoved into his pockets.

Gusts of wind whipped the lake water into waves. The sky grew even blacker.

"Now what?" I asked, my voice barely above a whisper.

"You have to go get it, Max," Tara said, wiping tears off her cheeks.

"Huh? Out in the middle of the lake?" I cried.

"If Mom and Dad are inside it . . ." Nicky's voice trailed off.

"We can't leave them at the bottom of the lake," Tara said. "We have to rescue them."

"But what if the pendant is empty?" I said. "What if it's just a pendant?"

They stared at me and didn't answer.

I knew the answer anyway. We had to make sure.

I wiped rainwater from my face. I gazed out onto the dark lake. "It's supposed to be filled with snakes," I said. "But it isn't true. I saw Colin and his friends swimming here. The rumors *can't* be true."

"I have my eye on the spot where the pendant landed," Tara said. "Go *now*, Max. Hurry. Get some goggles. Get a flashlight. You'll find it. I know you will." Her voice cracked.

"Great day for a swim," I said.

I turned and ran up the path to the cabins. My sneakers slid in the muddy grass. As I trotted by, I could hear the sound of the movie playing in the lodge.

Everyone else is dry and comfortable and having fun, I thought. And I'm going diving in that dark, creepy lake in a pounding rainstorm.

I was shivering as I pulled open the cabin door and stepped inside. The cabin smelled stale and moldy. Rain drummed on the flat roof, and water splashed down the windows.

My soaked sneakers squeaked on the floor-boards as I made my way to the chest where I kept my swimsuits.

"Hey, Max—what's up?"

The voice startled me. I jumped a mile.

Jakey gazed up at me from his bunk. He was sprawled on his back, reading a *manga* comic.

"Jakey, I didn't see you," I said, catching my breath. "What are you doing in here? Why aren't you watching the movie in the lodge?"

He shrugged. "Too scary. So I came back here."

I grabbed my swim trunks. Billy Wilbur had a pair of goggles hanging by his bunk. I grabbed them, too.

I pulled off my wet clothes and changed into the swim trunks.

"What are you doing?" Jakey asked, sitting up.

"Going for a swim," I said.

"But it's pouring!" he cried.

"I love swimming in the rain. It's my favorite," I lied. "Totally refreshing."

Jakey stared at me, frowning.

"Whenever it rains back home, I run out as fast as I can and go swimming," I said.

"Cool," he muttered. But I could see he didn't believe me.

I straightened the swim trunks. Pulled the goggles onto my forehead. And grabbed a waterproof flashlight off the shelf by the door.

"See ya," I called to Jakey.

He said something, but I was already out the door, back in the roar of the rain.

"Oh, wow!" I cried out as the cold water swept over my bare shoulders. I ran barefoot down the muddy path, splashing as I went.

Nicky and Tara were waiting at the shore. "Out there," Tara said, pointing. "Swim straight out, Max. Keep in a straight line from here, and you'll find it."

"Good luck," Nicky said, his voice a whisper in the roar of rain.

And then they both disappeared, leaving me alone on the shore. Shivering, I gripped the flashlight tightly as if hanging on to a life preserver.

With a trembling hand, I pulled the goggles down over my eyes. I clicked on the flashlight and sent a yellow beam of light out over the dark, tumbling water.

I thought about snakes. I couldn't help it.

I pictured them crawling along the muddy lake bottom. Fat, long snakes, their triangular heads raised as they slithered, tangling and untangling together. Tiny black eyes moving rapidly back and forth.

Waiting . . . watching for someone to swim by. Their jaws clamped tight . . . waiting . . . waiting for a chance to *snap*.

No. No way. Max, you saw the junior counselors swimming here. There are no dangerous snakes in Snake Lake.

I knew that was true. But I couldn't help thinking about them. I couldn't stop picturing them as I stepped into the lake.

My feet sank into the muddy bottom. The cold water washed over my ankles.

"Here goes," I muttered, and walked deeper into the dark water.

26

A FEW STEPS IN, the soft bottom dropped away. The water rose to my waist.

I stopped for a moment to catch my balance. The air was so cold, the lake water actually felt warm. The waves were gentle. They tickled my skin as they rolled past.

I bent my knees and dropped underwater. Something else tickled my skin.

Whoa. Wait.

Only lake grass. Remember the lake grass, Max. Don't panic.

I kept the flashlight close and beamed it straight down. Staring through the goggles, I could see the mud of the lake bottom and tiny plants rippling with the current.

I straightened up. Pushed off with both feet. And started to float.

It was hard to move forward with the flashlight gripped in one hand. I kicked hard and tried to float in a straight line.

Something tickled my leg. I turned and ducked

my head under the water. The flashlight beam fell on a cluster of snakelike weeds bobbing near the surface.

Stop thinking about snakes, Max, I told myself again.

The wind gusted hard. Rain washed into my face. I dove underwater, where it was calmer and warmer.

Floating facedown, I swept the light ahead of me. No sign of the pendant. The muddy bottom rippled and swirled beneath me.

I bobbed up and turned to shore. My eyes widened when I saw how far out I had swum.

Colin couldn't have thrown the pendant this far out. Should I swim back?

I gasped as something tickled my waist. I sank into the water, shining the light around frantically. A school of minnows fluttered past, shimmering like silver in the pale light.

Shimmering like little silver pods.

I kicked hard to move away from them. The water churned all around me. And when it settled once again, something else caught my beam of light—something that sparkled like silver!

My heart started to pound. Was that it? Had I found the pendant? The flashlight trembled in my hand, making the light shimmer wildly over the lake bottom.

I rose to the surface, took a deep breath, and

made a strong dive. Where was it? Where was that sparkly object? I moved the light in narrow circles over the mud and plants.

The light stopped at a white rock—a smooth white rock tucked into the lake-bottom mud. And resting on top of the rock . . . resting there as if someone had carefully placed it there—the *pendant*!

I was so excited, I opened my mouth, swallowed water, and started to choke.

The water tasted thick and sour in my mouth. I burst up to the surface, gasping and gagging. I pulled a clump of lake grass off my neck.

Finally, I started to breathe normally. But I couldn't get the sour taste from my mouth. I took a few deep breaths and plunged back underwater.

Yes. It was still there on the rock. A miracle. I had found it.

I wanted to leap up and down and pump my fists in the air. Nicky and Tara would be so happy!

The light trembled in front of me as I swam down toward the pendant. I made a grab for it, and it slid out of my hand.

My chest started to ache. I needed to take a breath. But I ignored the urgent feeling and shoved my hand forward. I wrapped my fingers tightly around the pendant.

Yes!

I had it. But my lungs felt ready to burst. I

kicked my way to the surface and floated there, gasping, sucking in breath after breath.

"I have it!" I shouted. I started waving it to Nicky and Tara. But I couldn't see them.

The rain had slowed a bit. I bobbed in the warm water, catching my breath. I gripped the pendant tightly in my hand and, squinting through the goggles, scanned the shore.

No sign of Nicky and Tara. The shore was empty. Beyond the shore, I could see lights flashing in the windows of the lodge.

The storm clouds had rolled on. The sky brightened to a light gray. But dark thoughts washed into my mind.

Was Phears waiting for me somewhere? When he saw that I had the pendant, would he show himself?

Would he *attack*?

I didn't want to think about that. I just wanted to solve the mystery of the pendant.

Nicky and Tara were so desperate to find their parents. We had been searching for them since October. Here it was July and maybe—just maybe—I held the answer in my hand.

I was still treading water, watching the shore—when I felt something soft wrap itself around one ankle.

"Hey—!" I let out a shout.

Something curled around my knee. Something

else slid around my waist. It felt like a leather belt, tightening . . . tightening . . .

"Hey—wait!"

Another belt tightened around my other ankle. I felt another one, a bigger one, wind around my waist.

I was kicking hard to stay afloat. I had the flashlight in one hand, the pendant in the other. It was awkward for me to turn. But I ducked my head into the water and twisted my body to see—

—*snakes!*

Long green snakes had wrapped around both my ankles. Two more were tightening around my waist. Despite the cold water, their bodies were warm.

"Help!" I forced myself higher in the water and let out a cry.

Where had they come from? From the muddy lake bottom? Were the stories about Snake Lake true after all?

I tried to call for help again. But the snakes around my ankles tugged hard. They were pulling me down!

I felt tingles of warmth as snakes circled my legs and began to tighten. Two snakes swam up the legs of my swim trunks. I could feel them wrapping around my thighs.

I sucked in a deep breath as the snakes began to pull me down.

As I sank, I let go of the flashlight. I thrashed on the surface with my free hand, struggling to stay above water.

The snakes tightened around me—around my waist, my legs, my ankles. And then I felt something warm slide around my throat.

It began to tighten. I was doomed.

I sucked in one more breath before my head slid under the water.

The snakes pulled me down, down to the muddy lake bottom.

And the pendant floated out of my hand. . . .

27

I KICKED AND THRASHED. The dark water churned around me.

My chest ached. I couldn't hold my breath much longer.

I twisted my body, trying to throw off the snakes. But they were too strong for me. They held on tightly, cutting into my skin, holding me underwater.

Something jerked my leg out from under me. I felt something grab my arm.

I had my eyes shut. I didn't see Nicky and Tara at first.

When I realized they were underwater with me—frantically trying to pry the snakes off—I nearly opened my mouth to shout for joy!

Nicky pulled a snake off my ankle, heaved it, and sent it floating away. Tara tore at the two snakes around my waist.

The ghosts looked solid, but the water seemed to flow right through them.

My chest throbbed with pain. My lungs felt about to explode.

99

My throat ached. I felt dizzy. The water churned around me. Around and around . . . till I closed my eyes again.

Please—I have to breathe!

Nicky tugged another snake off my leg. Then my two ghost friends grabbed my feet—and pushed. They gave me a hard shove to the surface.

My head popped out of the water. I opened my mouth and, choking and sputtering, let out a long whoosh of air and sucked in a fresh one.

Treading water, I waited for my heart to stop pounding. I waited for the ache in my chest to fade. Then I began half swimming, half floating to shore.

I felt totally drained. My arms and legs seemed to weigh a thousand pounds. The shore seemed a million miles away, but I pushed myself toward it.

I turned to float on my back for a while—and saw something shiny bobbing on the surface of the water. My heart skipped a beat. I turned and floated to the tiny object.

Just a leaf? A dead fish floating on its side?

No. The pendant . . . floating on a clump of weeds.

I wrapped my hand around it. This time, I wouldn't let go.

The rain had stopped. But the wind blew hard, cold against my face.

Gripping the pendant tightly, I made it to shore and pulled myself out of the water. Shivering in the cold air, I raised the pendant close to my face and rubbed the water off it with my finger.

Behind me, I could hear voices from the lodge. The other campers were still inside. The aroma of roasting chicken floated out from the mess hall kitchen.

Hugging myself to stop my shivers, I turned to the water and searched for Nicky and Tara.

Where were they? They should be on the shore by now.

The lake water stretched like an enormous black hole under the dark sky. I shuddered, thinking about the snakes again. My legs itched and tingled.

Deadly snakes. The camp story wasn't a joke. Snake Lake was filled with powerful snakes that could pull a camper down to the bottom and hold him there.

Then why were Colin and his friends swimming here?

I shook my head hard, sending a spray of water all around me. I didn't want to think about the snakes. Every time I pictured them wrapped around me, swimming up the legs of my swim trunks, my whole body started to tremble.

"Nicky? Tara? Where are you?" I called.

The dark water lapped quietly against the

shore. Somewhere in the trees, a bird uttered a hoarse caw.

"Nicky? Tara?"

Were they still underwater searching for the pendant?

I cupped both hands around my mouth. "I have it!" I screamed. "I have the pendant! Hey—I have it!"

No reply.

No sign of them. I squinted into the gray light and searched for them.

What's taking them so long? Why don't they come up from the lake?

28

I TRIED AGAIN. "I have the pendant!" I shouted. "Come out! I have the pendant!"

I watched the black water, low waves rolling to shore. All I could hear was the splash of the water and the rush of wind.

Finally, two pale shadows rose from the surface. All gray at first. Standing side by side, they floated toward me, a foot above the water.

A few seconds later, Nicky and Tara stood next to me. The water drained off them. In seconds, they were totally dry.

"Where were you?" I cried. "You scared me to death!"

Tara brushed back her dark hair. She straightened the dangling red earrings she wore. "Sorry, Max," she said.

"We were searching for the snakes," Nicky said. He pulled a clump of lake grass out of his jeans pocket and tossed it to the ground.

I stared at them. "Huh? Searching for snakes? Are you crazy? What are you talking about?"

103

"The snakes all vanished," Nicky said. "When Tara and I started to pull them off you, they vanished into thin air."

"They weren't real snakes," Tara said.

"They sure looked like snakes to me!" I said. "If they weren't snakes, what were they?"

"Ghosts, probably," Tara said.

The words hung in the air between us. We stared at each other without saying anything more.

Finally, I raised my hand. "The pendant!" I cried. "I have it!"

Tara let out a happy cry. She took it from my hand. She studied it, then gave it to Nicky. He turned it over and over.

"We have to be fast," Tara said. "Phears is here. He's waiting for this. If he sees that we have the pendant . . ."

"He wants to find Mom and Dad as much as we do," Nicky said, gazing at the pendant. "Because he wants to destroy them for good."

I took the pendant back. "What do we do?" I asked. "If your parents are inside this thing, how do we get them out?"

Tara sighed. "Good question," she said.

"There's no opening," I said. "It's sealed tight. There's no button to push. No lever or anything."

"Maybe we could smash it against a rock," Tara said. "Break it open."

"Maybe," I said. "But maybe if we got a screw-driver . . ."

Nicky took it back from me and studied it hard. "No place to put a screwdriver. No place to pry it open."

"Max? Hey, Max?" I heard a high voice from the path behind us. I spun around and saw Jakey running full speed toward us.

"Max? What's happening, Max?" he called.

"Stay away," I shouted. "It's dangerous here, Jakey. Go back to the lodge."

"But I'm afraid," he said. He kept coming. He ran right up to me.

"Jakey, please—" I begged.

"I'm afraid, Max," he said. "I'm afraid."

"Afraid of what?" I asked.

Jakey turned to Nicky. "I'm afraid you'll have to give me that," he said, and reached for the pendant.

29

I LET OUT A SHOCKED GASP. "You—you can *see* them?" I asked Jakey.

He ignored me and kept his hand outstretched in front of Nicky. His eyes were suddenly cold and gray. His mouth turned down in an ugly scowl.

"I'll take it," Jakey said softly. "Hand it over—now."

"No way!" Nicky exclaimed. "Back off, little boy."

Jakey made a grab for the pendant.

Nicky tossed it to me.

But his throw was high, and the pendant sailed over my shoulder.

It bounced into the mud. I spun around and dove for it.

Jakey dove at the same time. He landed hard on my back. Grunting loudly, we both stretched our hands for the pendant—

—and I came up with it!

I wrapped my fingers around it. Then I spun out from under Jakey and jumped to my feet.

His eyes on the pendant, Jakey took a few steps back. He was breathing hard, and his face turned bright red.

"You'll hand it over," he said through gritted teeth. "You'll *beg* me to take it from you."

I heard a cracking sound, like someone breaking an egg.

And then I gasped as Jakey's head started to split open. Narrow black veins crisscrossed his face. His eyes rolled up into his head. The cracking sound grew louder.

And his head broke apart!

"Oh no!" Tara pressed her hand to her mouth. Nicky stared, his jaw dropping.

I gripped the pendant tightly and watched in horror as Jakey's arms fell off. Part of his chest slid out from under his T-shirt.

His legs snapped and collapsed. The top of his head lay on the ground at his feet. His hands splintered and broke off from his arms, which were already on the ground.

Jakey broke into pieces.

Nothing left now but a shell. The trunk of his body stood upright in the lakeshore mud.

And then a black mist floated up from the trunk.

The black smoke smelled so sour, I held my nose. My eyes started to water.

I turned my head as the wind off the lake blew the disgusting smoke in my face.

When I turned back, I saw Nicky and Tara huddled together in fright.

And I saw a tall dark man wrapped in a black cloak, his face hidden in the swirling black mist. Hidden except for his ice white eyes, which were locked on mine.

Phears!

"Did you like my disguise, Max?" he boomed in a deep voice that rippled the lake. *"My way of staying close to you."*

I opened my mouth, but no sound came out.

"Did you forget that I am the Animal Traveler?" Phears bellowed. *"Humans* are animals too." He snickered—an ugly dry laugh.

"You—you killed Jakey!" I cried.

He shook his head. "There never was a Jakey. My magic is stronger than you know."

Then Phears stuck his hand out from the mist. "Enough talk. *Hand it over,*" he growled. *"Now."*

30

I STARED UP AT PHEARS, my whole body trembling. He floated away from the chunks of Jakey on the ground.

He held his hand out. "Now, Max. Hand over the life pod."

My mind whirred. I knew I couldn't fight him. I remembered the pain he'd caused me before. How he'd peeled back my fingernails and the skin on my hands. How he'd drilled all my teeth at once until I howled in agony.

I knew he could do that to me again if I didn't cooperate.

So I didn't hesitate for long. As Phears loomed over me, hand outstretched, I raised the pendant to him.

And then I heard Tara's shout. "Keepaway! Keepaway, Max!"

I pulled my hand back—and tossed the pendant to her.

Phears uttered an angry growl. The swirling black mist followed him as he spun toward Tara.

Tara tossed the pendant to Nicky. Nicky grabbed it in one hand and started running along the shore.

"Hand it over!" Phears demanded. He dove at Nicky.

Nicky leaped out of Phears' grasp. Nicky's feet slipped on the muddy ground, and he started to fall. As he fell, he heaved the pendant to me.

A wild throw.

Phears let out another angry growl.

The pendant sailed over my head. I leaped high but couldn't bring it down.

I turned in time to see it crash into a white rock near the water.

It made a loud *clink*. The sound echoed in my ears.

I froze and stared as the pendant split apart.

A bright flash of light made me shut my eyes.

When I opened them again, I saw the two halves of the pendant slide off the rock.

And then a thick white mist rose high into the sky. It swirled in a funnel shape, like a white cyclone, rising higher, bright against the gray sky.

It spun faster and faster. We all stared up at the whirling white funnel cloud.

I let out a gasp as two figures floated out of the cloud.

They floated quickly down to the ground. A man and a woman, both wearing white lab coats. Blinking in the light, they gazed around in confusion.

And as they landed in front of us, I recognized them. Recognized them from Nicky and Tara's framed photograph.

"Mom! Dad!" Nicky screamed.

"I *knew* you were in there!" Tara cried.

31

NICKY AND TARA RAN forward to hug their parents.

I stood back and watched them hugging and crying, all talking at once. I realized I had tears in my eyes too. I felt as happy as Nicky and Tara.

We'd spent so many months searching for Mr. and Mrs. Roland. And I'd been wearing the pendant the whole time!

"We told you we were close," Mr. Roland said, hugging Nicky and Tara for the fifth time. "Which one of you found the life pod?"

Tara pointed to me. "That's our friend, Max. He lives in our old house. He's been helping us search for you. We figured out that you were inside the life pod he wore."

"Thank you for being their friend," Mrs. Roland said to me, wiping tears off her cheeks with both hands.

"A ghost named Phears destroyed our lives," Mr. Roland explained. "He destroyed our lab. He destroyed our family. Then he locked us inside a life pod. We—"

He stopped talking as a deep voice boomed from behind us on the shore. "I hate to break up this happy family reunion," Phears said, half hidden in his cloak of black fog. "I've been waiting for this moment a long time."

"Phears!" Mr. Roland shouted, wrapping his arms around Nicky and Tara. "Haven't you done enough evil?"

"Can't you leave our family alone?" Mrs. Roland demanded, her dark eyes flashing angrily.

"You didn't leave *me* alone!" Phears screamed in a sudden rage. "You two locked my friends and me up in those pods. You said you were ridding the world of evil spirits."

Phears floated closer, close enough so that we could see the anger in his solid white eyes. "You call yourselves scientists," he raged. "I call you *murderers*. You had no right to invade the tunnel between the living and the dead. No right to set up your lab to capture ghosts. No right to meddle in the spirit world."

"Your evil had to be stopped," Mr. Roland said, holding on to Nicky and Tara.

A cold grin crossed Phears' face. "But you *didn't* stop me. I escaped. And I helped to free all the other ghostly spirits you unjustly captured."

"Leave us alone!" Tara shouted. "Just go away and leave us alone!"

Phears ignored her. "I locked the two of you in a life pod," he continued. "I tried to hide the pod. I tossed it in your house. I always meant to come back and finish you off. Finish you. Yes, finish you."

He sighed. "But it took me all this time to get you all together."

"Run!" Tara screamed. She gave her mom and dad a shove. "Come on—run!"

Phears tossed back his head in a cruel laugh. "You can't escape!" he bellowed. "I have you out-numbered!"

Phears waved a hand over his head. I heard a rumbling sound. At first, I thought it was thunder far in the distance.

A loud splash made me turn to the lake. A high wave crashed against the shore. The lake erupted in tall waves, smashing against each other.

Another roar like thunder, much louder and closer.

And then I turned to the tossing, crashing waters. And saw a scene of total horror!

Curling on itself, snapping its jaws, a gray-green snake floated up from the waves. And then another, right beneath it.

The snakes uncurled and raised their heads with a loud hiss.

As I watched frozen in disbelief, snake after snake flew up from the lake. Their jaws snapped open and shut. Their hisses drowned out the crashing of the waves.

A solid *wall* of twisting, hissing snakes, rising from beneath the water.

The snakes rose higher and higher. . . . The hissing, wriggling wall reached to the sky.

As the wall of snakes loomed over us, they began to crack apart. The hissing grew deafening, like an explosion that didn't end. I had to cover my ears.

And then the hissing was replaced by the howl of ghosts. Black smoke poured out of the open snakes, poured out until it formed a black storm cloud over our heads.

Behind the black cloud, the snake bodies fell back into the water. As they hit the surface, they didn't make a sound. Hundreds of snake bodies slid into the lake, silently, without a splash.

And then the waves stopped crashing. The lake turned calm and flat again. No sign of the phantom snakes anywhere. The water lapped the shore gently, as if nothing had happened.

And out of the thick black cloud of smoke came an army of Phears' ghosts.

I trembled all over and my teeth started to chatter as I stared up at them. Shadowy men and women dressed in gray. Dull eyes and dead faces, blank and lifeless.

They moved together like zombies—an army of the dead. They floated down from the black cloud with their hands at their sides, their bodies stiff, their eyes straight ahead.

Phears waved his hands again. The ghosts all landed at the same time. They swept past me. Floated right through me.

I could hear them jabbering to themselves. They murmured excitedly without moving their gray lips. They were excited about capturing Nicky and Tara and their parents.

Another command from Phears, and the jabbering ghosts surrounded the Rolands. They formed a tight circle around them.

I couldn't see them now. I stood helplessly watching the ghostly circle.

And then I heard Tara's voice, muffled by the evil bodies. "Max—help! Help us!"

32

THE WALL OF GRAY GHOSTS parted for a brief moment. I saw four ghosts holding Mr. and Mrs. Roland down. Two other ghosts had Nicky's and Tara's arms pinned behind their backs.

"Max—the pendant!" Mr. Roland shouted. "Put it back together. It's our only chance."

I turned and saw the two pieces of the pendant glimmering beside the rock on the shore. My legs were trembling. It seemed to take forever to get them to move.

Finally, I took off running toward the pendant.

I felt a cold wind on the back of my neck. Glancing behind me, I saw Phears, floating fast, coming after me.

With a loud cry, I dove for the pendant pieces. Grabbed them in one hand. "I've got it!" I groaned.

And then I cried out in pain as Phears' heavy, pointed boot kicked the pieces out of my hand.

The pieces of the pendant flew to the mud.

Howling, I shook my hand hard, trying to force away the pain.

Phears lowered himself to the ground and grabbed for the halves of the pendant.

I leaped onto his back.

Groaning, kicking and slapping at each other, we wrestled in the mud. His body was sticky and hot. His back felt hard, like the shell of a turtle.

His clothes were damp, and a slimy goo came off onto my body as I struggled with him. We rolled over and over in the mud.

Finally, he rolled on top of me. Sat heavily on my chest. And stared down at me in a rage. Those white eyes burned right through me.

And he bellowed, "You *dare* to challenge me? I'm going to turn you inside out now—like your dog!"

I felt a hard pull on my skin. The skin of my face started to pull back. My lips stretched back over my teeth.

He was doing it. Holding me down, he was pulling my skin back on itself, turning me inside out.

"No!" I spun around. Facedown, I tried to get a good grip on the ground. Tried to push him off me.

My hand felt something hard in the mud. Something metallic.

Yes! I wrapped my fingers around both pieces of the life pod.

Twisting my body, I freed my other hand.

My head throbbed. The skin of my face pulled tighter.

With a frantic swing, I brought my hands together. And shoved the two halves of the pendant shut. Back in one piece.

It clicked into place.

I heard the *click*—and then, with a high scream that shook the trees, Phears flew up into the sky—and vanished.

My skin slid back over my teeth. Still on my back, I stared up at the clouds. No Phears. He really was gone.

Panting, I climbed to my knees. I held the pendant high. "I've got the pendant back together!" I choked out. "Hey, I've got it!"

At the sound of my voice, the ghosts all spun away from the Rolands. Jabbering, their dead eyes locked on me, they came rushing forward. Stampeding toward me. A wall of gray dead-faced ghosts, storming at me, muttering excitedly.

Coming to finish me off.

I fought off my panic and jumped to my feet. I turned and started to run.

But my feet slipped in the wet mud. I went down face-first.

I fell hard. Pain shot through my body. But I held on to the pendant.

No time to climb back up. No time . . .

The jabbering ghosts swarmed over me.

33

I STRUGGLED TO MY KNEES as the first ghost attacked.

A whoosh of cold, sour air blew over me. The ghost's long gray hair flew up behind his head. His mouth was open in a silent scream. His bony, pale arms reached out, fingers cracking.

And then he was gone.

It took me a few seconds to realize that he had vanished into the life pod.

The pod trembled in my hand as I held it in front of me.

With a strong blast of air, another ghost disappeared inside it. And then another.

The pod bounced and jerked in my hand. I tightened my fist and held on.

The trees rang with the screams and wails of the ghostly army. They raised their hands as shields and struggled to hang back.

But the pod acted like a powerful vacuum cleaner. Its pull proved too strong for them. One by one, it sucked them inside.

The ghosts were gone in minutes. My hand trembled and vibrated. The air still smelled sour with the sick smell of death.

Mr. Roland took the pendant from me and pressed it tight. "Thank you, Max," he said, waving it in front of him. A tense smile spread over his face. "Now they're back where they belong."

Mrs. Roland had her arms around Nicky and Tara.

"And where do *we* belong, Dad?" Tara asked in a trembling voice.

Mr. Roland sighed. "I wish I knew."

"We have to start all over again," Mrs. Roland said. "If we can rebuild our lab, maybe we can find a way to be solid again."

"You mean maybe we can be alive?" Tara asked.

"Maybe," Mrs. Roland murmured.

"At least we captured the ghosts," Mr. Roland said.

"All except Phears," I said.

That made everyone stop. We all glanced around the camp. A chill tightened the back of my neck.

Phears could still be lurking.

"Let's move on before Phears returns," Mr. Roland said. He raised the life pod. "I want to hide these ghosts away somewhere safe, where no one will ever find them again."

We turned away from the lake and began walking toward the lodge. The sky brightened. A hazy sun poked through the parting clouds.

Mrs. Roland walked with her arms around Nicky and Tara. Their father had a grim, determined look on his face. He held the life pod tightly in his hand.

I saw something gleaming on top of an evergreen shrub. A large caterpillar. The sunlight caught it and made it shine.

As I started to move past it, I saw the caterpillar grow.

In seconds, it had puffed itself up to the size of a hot dog. A prickly green hot dog. I stopped with a sharp gasp. I knew what was happening.

The caterpillar curled on top of the shrub. Soon it was as long and fat as a baseball bat.

"Hey—" I called to the Rolands up ahead of me. "Hey, it's—it's—"

My warning came too late.

I fell back, startled, as the caterpillar burst apart with a loud *pop*. Its guts flew from its shattered body. The hot and sticky yellow glop splashed me in the face and covered my hair.

"Ohhh." I let out a moan and frantically tried to wipe the disgusting stuff away.

When I raised my eyes, Phears floated out from the exploded caterpillar. I watched helplessly as his swirling black fog encircled Mr. Roland.

Mr. Roland had no time to put up a struggle. Phears grabbed the life pod from his hand.

Then Phears floated over us, and his laughter boomed through the trees.

"Like taking candy from a baby," he said.

34

BEAMS OF SUNLIGHT TRICKLED through Phears' black fog, though his face remained hidden in darkness. But we didn't need to see his face to know that he was smiling.

He floated over the Rolands, waving the life pod, teasing them with it. "Phears wins," he said. "Phears wins. You lose."

"Take it and leave!" Mr. Roland shouted up to him. "We won't go after you, Phears. Take your ghost friends with you and go away."

"I have a better plan," Phears replied. "I let my friends out now. I put the four of you inside. *Then* I leave."

He snickered. "A much better plan. And this time I'll find a cozier hiding place for the Roland family. Someplace where you can enjoy being together forever."

He turned his gaze on me. "Don't think I've forgotten you, Max. Don't worry. I'll think of a good ending for you, too."

I hurried up to the Rolands. "Is there anything

124

I can do?" I whispered. "Is there any way Phears can be destroyed?"

Silence for a long moment.

Then Mrs. Roland whispered, "Only one way he can be destroyed. He teased us with it when we first captured him. He can only be destroyed by someone shouting out his real name."

"But no one knows it," Mr. Roland added. "And no one has ever been able to guess it."

I gazed up into Phears' swirling mist. *His real name? Phears' real name?*

What could it be?

Above us, Phears leaned out from his fog cloud. I could see his dark cloak and, above it, his pale face with its eerie white eyes. He held the pod in front of him and prepared to open it and release his ghostly friends.

What could his name be? What?

And suddenly, I knew. Suddenly, I figured it out.

"I have it!" I shouted. "I think I know his real name!"

35

I WAS TREMBLING all over. I knew I had only one chance to save the Roland family—and to save myself!

I cupped my hands around my mouth, cleared my throat, and forced a shout.

"Seraph!" I screamed. "Your name is *Seraph!"*

"Seraph" means "angel."

And "seraph" is an anagram of "Phears."

Angel is the *last* thing Phears would want to be called.

But was it his real name?

"Seraph!" I screamed one more time.

At the sound of the name, Phears opened his mouth in a high wail of horror. It sounded like a dozen ambulance sirens screaming above us.

And then he blew apart. His head flew off first—and exploded in a burst of red and yellow goo. And then his arms and legs shot off his body and disintegrated into powder.

His body floated by itself for a moment. Then it

turned brown and closed in on itself, like a marsh-mallow burning in a campfire.

And then the sky was clear, except for a few lingering wisps of black fog, floating in the bright sunlight.

"Max, you're a genius!" Tara cried. She and Nicky hurried over to hug me. Then we began jumping up and down for joy.

"Phears is destroyed," Mr. Roland said. "Gone forever."

See? My word games came in handy! What a shame I couldn't tell anyone about this. Who would believe it?

"Oh, look. We're fading away," Mrs. Roland said. "All this excitement has drained our energy."

She was right. All four of them were flickering like fireflies.

"I guess we have to say goodbye," Mr. Roland said. "Goodbye and thank you, Max."

"We'll never forget you," Tara said.

"Have a nice life," Nicky said.

"I'll . . . miss you," I choked out.

More hugs. More tears.

And then they were gone.

I stood blinking in the bright sunlight. A wave of sadness swept over me. What will my life be like without Nicky and Tara? I wondered.

For the first time, I realized they were my best friends.

And I had just lost my best friends forever.

I turned and saw Uncle Joey standing in front of me, hands on his hips. "Max, what's up? Why aren't you in the lodge with everyone else?" he asked. "What are you doing out here?"

"Not much," I replied. "Just making up anagrams."

Was I happy to get home?

I practically kissed the floor. I was so happy that camp was over, I was even glad to see Buster. He greeted me with a growl and snapped at my fingers. Good old Buster!

Mom and Dad were happy to have Colin and me back. As I headed up to my room to start unpacking my stuff, Mom handed me a slice of my favorite cake.

"See? Camp wasn't as bad as you thought it would be, was it, Maxie?" she asked.

"No. It was much worse," I replied.

I had to tell the truth, right?

I took the plate of cake and hurried upstairs.

"What took you so long?" a voice demanded as I stepped into my room.

"Where've you been?" another voice asked.

Nicky and Tara appeared. "We've been waiting for days," Tara said.

I let out a cry and nearly dropped the cake.

"But—but—" I sputtered. "What are you doing here?"

"Mom and Dad thought we'd be safer here," Nicky said. "They're going to rebuild their ghost-catching lab. Someplace secret. And they're going to try to learn how we can all be solid again—not ghosts."

"But it might be really dangerous," Tara said. "So they told us to wait for them here."

"Guess we'll be haunting you for a while," Nicky said.

"Huh? For how long?" I asked.

They both shrugged. "Who knows?"

Tara grabbed the plate of cake from my hands. "My favorite!" she cried. "And I'm so totally hungry!"

"Whoa. So am I!" Nicky said. He grabbed the cake from Tara's hand.

The cake was flying back and forth when Colin burst into my room. "Max—?" He started to ask me something, but he stopped when he saw the cake.

"Max? That cake—it's flying back and forth by itself!"

"Of course," I said. "It's *angel* food cake."

ABOUT THE AUTHOR

Robert Lawrence Stine's scary stories have made him one of the bestselling children's authors in history. "Kids like to be scared!" he says, and he has proved it by selling more than 300 million books. R.L. teamed up with Parachute Press to create Fear Street, the first and number one bestselling young adult horror series. He then went on to launch Goosebumps, the creepy bestselling series that gave kids chills all over the world and made him the number one children's author of all time (*The Guinness Book of Records*).

R.L. Stine lives in Manhattan with his wife, Jane, their son, Matthew, and their dog, Nadine. He says he has never seen a ghost—but he's still looking!

Check out the next book in R.L. Stine's
Mostly Ghostly series:

GHOULS GONE WILD

MAX'S PARENTS ARE PLANNING to sell their house
and move the family far, far away. Max has to
stop them! He can't leave Nicky and Tara, the
two ghosts who live with him. They need him.
He's the only one who can help them become real
kids again!

But Max has another problem right now—a
figure dressed in black, with a face hidden in
shadow. It's a boy—or is it? That's what Max needs
to know, because this shadowy figure is following
him. Watching him. Waiting for him . . .

GHOULS GONE WILD
Coming in April 2005!

ON SATURDAY AFTERNOON, I walked over to see my best friend, Aaron, to tell him the bad news. I knew he'd be upset about my family moving away.

It was going to be really tough for both of us. For one thing, Aaron had *Buffy,* Season One, and I had *Buffy,* Season Two. How would we ever trade episodes?

Aaron greeted me at the door and led me to his room. He closed the door behind us. "Shhhh." He put a finger to his lips. "I brought home a jar of honey."

I squinted at him. "Honey? Why?"

"I'm going to pour it into my sister's bed," he whispered.

"Why?" I asked.

"Revenge," he said.

Aaron spends a big part of every day getting revenge on his six-year-old sister, Kaytlin.

Aaron giggled. "Tonight she'll climb into bed. She won't see the honey till it's too late. She'll be sticky for the rest of her life." He giggled some more.

"I came over to tell you something," I said.

"Shhhh. Not now," he whispered. "I'll show you the jar of honey." He grabbed his backpack and pulled it open.

His mouth dropped open and his eyes bulged. He let out a groan. "Oh, noooo."

I peered into the backpack. The lid had come off the jar. The thick, sticky honey had spilled all over Aaron's books and binders.

He lifted his math book out. It was dripping with a heavy layer of gunk.

"Ruined," Aaron moaned. "I'm ruined." He dropped the soaked textbook into the backpack. "Kaytlin did this!" he cried, shaking a fist. "She did this. This means *war*!"

"But, Aaron, I need to tell you something," I said.

He tossed the backpack down and flew out the door. I followed him to the kitchen. He pulled open a food cabinet and began shoving jars and bottles out of his way.

"Here it is," he said. He held up a jar. "Honey. We haven't lost. This war is just beginning."

"*We?*"

He pulled off the lid and tossed it aside. Then he ran past me with the jar raised in front of him. His eyes were wild. His mouth was pulled back in an evil villain's grin.

I followed him back down the long hall. He

stopped at his sister's room and peeked in. "She's not home," he said. "Come on." He tiptoed to Kaytlin's dresser. He slid open the top drawer. He giggled. "It's her underwear drawer. Check it out."

I didn't really want to see Kaytlin's underwear. But I didn't have a choice. I peeked into the drawer.

Her underpants were neatly folded and in rows, organized by color.

I tried again. "Aaron, I really have to tell you something."

But he motioned for me to hush. Then he held the honey jar over the drawer and tipped it upside down. Slowly, slowly, the thick gloop started to pour out, onto Kaytlin's underpants.

Aaron moved the jar slowly back and forth. He had covered two rows of underpants when his mother stepped into the room.

"Aaron? What on earth are you doing?" she asked.

Aaron turned around, the jar still over the drawer. "Uh . . . nothing," he said.

"You are going to be doing nothing for a long, long time," she said. "Because you are grounded for life."

"Not again," Aaron said.

So I had to leave. I didn't have a chance to tell Aaron my sad news. I decided I'd e-mail him when I got home.

The sun had gone down. Dark storm clouds hung low in the sky. The wind howled around me as I started to walk the two blocks to my house.

I kept my head down and walked with my hands in my pockets. How did it suddenly get so cold?

I'd only gone past a few houses when I heard a scraping sound behind me.

I spun around. Was someone there?

I saw a blur of motion. Something moved behind a low hedge. I shrugged and started walking again. But now I was listening carefully.

And again, I heard a scrape. A few soft thuds. The sounds of footsteps.

Someone was definitely following me.

I stopped. And the sounds behind me stopped, too.

I spun around again. Hard to see anything in this pitch-black night.

The dark clouds seemed to lower over me. The wind howled, shaking the trees.

A chill tightened the back of my neck.

I heard a cough. From behind a nearby pine tree.

"Aaron?" I called, shouting over the wind. "Hey—Aaron? Is that you?"

A head poked out from behind the tree.

I squinted through the heavy darkness, trying to see the face.

A boy?

He stepped away from the tree. Yes. A boy. Dressed all in black. Creepy.

He took a few steps toward me. His face was hidden in shadow.

I turned and started to run. I could hear his pounding footsteps. He was chasing me! What did he want? I didn't stop to find out. Gasping for breath, I forced myself to run harder.

I ducked my head as large raindrops began to patter down. The sidewalk ended. I darted across the street. Only half a block to go.

I heard the boy's footsteps on the pavement behind me. He was catching up. Leaning forward, I tried to lay on more speed.

And then I let out a cry as my shoes slid out from under me. No way to stop myself. I fell hard. Fell facedown. Into a deep muddy trench.

"Owww!" I landed hard. Gasping, choking, I struggled to my knees. And stared up at the boy in black, faceless, his head covered in darkness.

"Who are you?" I cried. "What do you want?"

Silence. He didn't move. The only sounds now were my wheezing breaths and the hard patter of raindrops all around.

And then finally, the boy whispered, whispered in a low, hoarse voice, *"I'm watching.... I'm watching...."*